This book is dedicated to

The Reverend Doctor James Dale Abel,

Pastor, Mentor, Colleague, and most importantly, Friend

ACKNOWLEGMENTS

This book would not have come to be had it not been for the people mentioned below. I am grateful for their help.

To: Miriam Chapman to be the first person to read the draft, make many important suggestions and for being the cheer leader to encourage me to continue the process of publishing.

To: Kristin Voyles for proofing and editing the manuscript, serving as my personal IT consultant and for being a muse and mentor in how to express my thoughts.

To: Jeanne Jeffrey and CPT (USN-RET) Dan V. Kral for proofing the manuscript and making many helpful suggestions.

To: Dave Holland, MD and Mike Zlomke, MD for providing much needed consultation on medical terms and treatments.

To: Viviananna Ayuso for correcting *mi español malo.*

To: Those who saw things in the book I didn't and were willing to write "A Praise" about it.

To: John Hornbeak, FACHE, the best boss I ever had.

To: Jean Tennant, Shapato Publishing, for her encouragement and initial editing.

To: Neal Wooten, Mirror Publishing, for his patience, guidance and willingness to put up with me.

Through the Valley

A Novel

By

Michael T. Curd, D. Min.

ISBN 978-1-61225-237-7

Published by Mirror Publishing
Milwaukee, WI 53214
www.pagesofwonder.com

Printed in the USA

PRAISE FOR THROUGH THE VALLEY

Michael Curd submerges his readers into the world of hospital chaplaincy in all its drama and tragedy from start to finish. His story presents an authentic journey of spiritual call and purpose through the eyes of the pastoral staff in a medical center. Readers will share in their emotional ride in the fast-paced and shockingly blunt medical novella. Engaging and enlightening.

--- The Reverend Jane Florence, D. Min., Senior Pastor, FUMC, Omaha, Nebraska

During my 24 year career as a U.S. Army Chaplain, Mike Curd had the reputation as being the best trauma caregiver in the active duty military chaplaincy. Through the Valley, which I know personally, is an autobiographical novel, is the finest anecdotal depiction I have read about effective trauma care ministry in a clinical setting. For all those who seek to be a healing presence through appropriate and effective pastoral care, this book clearly points the way. All pastoral caregivers would do well to read it often and keep it close at hand.

--- Chaplain (Colonel-Retired) C. Dennis Camp

I found Through the Valley to be a candidly refreshing view into the real world of hospital chaplains. This kind of intense honesty can only be conveyed by one who has lived and worked in the trenches of a hectic urban health care system with its round the clock drama and pathos. One can palpably sense the fatigue and sorrow; yet pervading throughout is a deep sense of faith in, and dependence on Divine Power for the strength to continue onward. I cannot too highly recommend this book for its insights into the daily walk of hospital chaplains and the wonderful difference they make in the lives of hurting people.

--- Miriam Chapman, RHIA, CPC, VA Medical Center, Omaha, Nebraska.

Charles S. Kemp, PhD, Distinguished Professor of Pastoral Care, Brite Divinity School, gifted pastor and professor, said that his favorite verses in the Bible are, "...And this shall come to pass...not staying forever...." Everyone walks through the valley. Dr. Curd helps the reader discover the compass suited for such aid. A tool helpful for everyone, his writing enables us to see how God's grace is appropriated in our most gutsy and bloody trips. Dr. Curd will give you new light for this important journey. I encourage you to obtain this compass.

--- The Reverend James D. Abel, D. Min., Fort Worth, Texas

Dr. Michael T. Curd uses unique descriptive language in his writing which adds delight to the reading! In addition, it is refreshing to be spiritually uplifted by this novel—through the spreading of the Gospel by people who exhibit great care for those most vulnerable. A good read!

--- Jean Sitter, RSM, Spiritual Director, Omaha, Nebraska

From his vast personal experiences as a chaplain, Michael draws out the true nature of this vital ministry. But what I appreciate most is his willingness to show the "real inside" of a chaplain, with all the natural needs, feelings, insecurities and human thoughts as well as the irony that the more real they allow themselves to be, while self reflective, the healthier they are as chaplain to others. A great message for all who are in any form of ministry or helping professions!

--- The Reverend Bill Selby, M.S., M. Div., President, Center for Pastoral Effectiveness of the Rockies, Highlands Ranch, Colorado

Through the Valley is riveting, exciting, slightly scandalous (in a delicious way) and very informative. I found myself caught up in the story line and anxious to know how it played out. It shed a beautiful light on something not many people know: The important, redemptive and often misunderstood work of clinical chaplains. It made me proud to have had the chance to serve as one. The depth of self-reflection in the characters was impressive, almost exhausting. I also enjoyed the mix of Spanish and English and all the references to Texas history and culture.

--- The Reverend Kara James, M. Div., BCC, Pastor of Congregational Care, St. Mark's UMC, Lincoln, Nebraska

Through the Valley by Michael T. Curd is an authentic look at the life of chaplains in a major healthcare system. Dr. Curd has drawn on his experience as a clinically trained chaplain in military and civilian hospitals and in the U.S. Army to paint a vivid picture of the challenges chaplains face and the wide range of activities encompassed by the simple job description of "Chaplain."

--- Lynn Irby, PhD, author, Bozeman, Montana

CHAPTER 1

31/1705 December 2005

"Trauma team to the trauma room. Trauma team to the trauma room." The pager went off as the last syllable of the PA system's metallic voice faded. Chaplain (Resident) Jaime Martinez's, adrenalin began to surge through his body. He had to consciously will himself to breathe in a semi-normal pattern, as he reached the stairwell on the fifth floor of Mercy Methodist Hospital. He took the stairs as quickly as he deemed safe, hurrying to the ground floor where the Level 1 trauma center was encased in the ER. His mind was a cacophony of memories: Naked bodies, blood, severed limbs, orders barked, CPR, defibrillation, tears and the hollow laughter of gallows humor.

What would it be this time? GSW, MVA, pedestrian versus car? thought Jaime.

"I've got my RN, LVN, my recorder, Docs, RT, X-ray. Where's my chaplain?" the trauma manager said in a loud voice.

"Chaplain's here!" Jaime said in an identical tone and volume as he walked through the door of Trauma Room B. The eight people wearing plastic aprons, protective glasses and latex gloves simultaneously gave a sigh of relief.

"EMS is five minutes out, Padre," said the recorder. Jaime nodded as he began putting on the universal precautions. He'd been on duty ten hours and had already handled two deaths and a Code Blue (Cardiac Arrest) while making rounds throughout the six hundred twenty-five bed hospital. He was tired. He was also pumped. He loved the rush of a trauma, which often caused him a wave of guilt.

The ambulance bay doors slid open as two EMTs pushed a gurney with a "packaged patient" on it. Jaime stepped out of the way as they moved into the room. *EMS never gets here as late as they say they will,* Jaime thought to himself. The ambulance gurney and the trauma gurney were married as, on the count of the doctor, the patient was transferred to the one belonging to the hospital.

One EMT gave report as they walked through the doors describing the patient, her list of injuries and the mechanism thereof. "Twenty-five year old Hispanic female, single car rollover MVA, restrained. BP 185 over 110, pulse 95, compound fracture of right femur and chest contusions. Alert and conscious times three. No LOC."

No loss of consciousness in a rollover motor vehicle accident, thought the young chaplain resident to himself. *That's a bit unusual.*

Thaddeus T. Washington, MD, spoke to the patient as other staff members began cutting off her clothes. As the EMTs' gurney was taken out of the room, Jaime moved to the head of the patient and waited for the physician to finish his questions about allergies, medical history and whether or not she had lost consciousness.

"Buenas tardes. Me llama Jaime y soy un capellán para el hospital." The woman's eyes began to widen, "And they call me for all of these. I'm part of the trauma team and we're going to take really good care of you. Tell me what happened."

"I don't speak Spanish," she said with a mixture of defiance and guilt. "Why are they cutting off my clothes? I'm okay. Don't cut my clothes. Please. I can take them off if I have to. Don't cut them."

"Tell me your name."

"Cynthia. Cynthia Gonzalez. Please don't cut my clothes off."

Jaime saw she was wearing a designer dress and her makeup appeared to be done by a professional, although it was a bit splotchy from the rain. She was very pretty. "I'm sorry, Cynthia, but we have to cut them off so you don't have to move. If you have a spinal injury and move around, it could make your injuries much worse. We want you to be safe."

"I don't have a spinal injury. I'm okay. You don't need to cut off my clothes," said Cynthia as she began to weep, quietly. Her bra and panties were cut and removed. She was completely naked, shaking from the cold and the embarrassment. The tears rolled down the sides of her face as she looked at the ceiling, as though hoping this would all go away.

"I know this is difficult and embarrassing, but we have to do it this way." Jaime said in a calm voice. "Tell me what happened, Cynthia."

"I was driving to my friend's house, down 281 and as I went around the curve just south of Basse Road I lost control. I don't know what happened next. The car just rolled over and over. Then it stopped and I was hanging upside down."

"Tell me what happened then."

"I felt the rain on my face because the window was gone. A man ran up to the car and asked if I was alright. I told him I didn't know, but I thought so. Then I saw some blood drip onto the roof lining." She closed her eyes as if trying not to see it again.

"Chaplain, we're going to do IVs and a femoral stick," said Renee Thompson, RN. She was all business with kind eyes. Twenty years in the ER had taught her many things and she had learned that letting the chaplain be the "interpreter" for the staff and tell the patient what was about to happen made the patient less anxious.

The first time, it was spontaneous. Prior to that, the patient heard a disembodied voice yell above the noise, "You're going to feel a stick," or worse. The change in function enabled the other staff to do their job more effectively without having to "fight the patient" in order to do a procedure. "Chappie" kept them calm which resulted in a quicker resuscitation and usually less stressed staff.

Jaime looked into Cynthia's eyes and said calmly, "You are going to feel a couple of little sticks, one in each hand. They need to get some IVs going to make sure you have plenty of fluids on board and they can give you the appropriate medications when the time comes. Tell me the thoughts you were having as the accident occurred."

"I thought I was going to die!" she said, her eyes getting larger. She looked like a frightened child. "May I touch your shoulder?" Jaime asked. She nodded. He gently touched her bare shoulder as he said, "That must have been scary."

Nodding, Cynthia began to cry again. Jaime said nothing. He increased the pressure on her shoulder slightly, as the tears flowed. Then she let out a scream! "It hurts, it hurts, make them stop."

"They had to reposition your leg. Next time they'll tell us before they do something," Jaime said as he glared at the newest staff member, Dr. Karl Sassmann, who said I'm sorry with his eyes, and continued his work. A slight smile crossed Renee's face as she turned to get a large, needled syringe and some four by four gauze pads. "We're going to do the femoral stick now, Padre."

He looked at Cynthia again and said, "You're going to feel a stick in your groin. They have to draw some blood."

"Why do they have to get it there? Can't they get it out of one of the IVs?" she said pleadingly.

"I wish they could, but it's better if it comes from there."

Dr. Washington broke the chain of his constant direction of the staff to tell Cynthia why it was better to get the blood from the femoral artery. Just as quickly, he resumed giving orders to the staff.

"Tell me the other thoughts you had." Jaime said softly.

"I couldn't believe it was happening. The men said it was best to wait for the ambulance before they tried to get me out. It was raining pretty hard. I heard the siren and in a few minutes the EMTs were getting me out and putting me on this board. They put this collar on me and then taped my head to the board. The rain was hitting me in the eyes, so I had to keep them closed. Then they put me into the ambulance and brought me here."

"That must have all been frightening." She nodded as Jaime asked, "Have you ever been in an ambulance before?"

"No. I didn't like it. On the way here, my leg started to hurt, really bad. Can they give me something for the pain? It still hurts."

10

"Not right now. They have to finish their assessment. If they give you pain meds now, it might mask an internal injury that you have. The accident was serious and they have to be certain of what injuries you have." Jaime looked at her to see if she understood what he had said. She nodded again, with new tears welling in her eyes.

"Okay, we need to roll her. Padre, can you help?" asked Dr. Washington. I've got her head; you take her shoulder, Renee, take the back and pelvis. New guy, what's your name? You get her leg, and try not to kill her this time. On my count, *uno, dos*, three. The team gently rolled her on her left side as the resident II, Dr. Hector Gutierrez, examined her back, buttocks and legs. She let out a moan as she was rolled onto her back, again.

"I can't breathe, I can't breathe," exclaimed Cynthia as she gasped for air.

"Doctor, her sats (oxygen level in the blood) are dropping," said Renee.

"She's got a pnuemo. Dr. Gutierrez, start a chest tube, stat," said Washington. The medical resident II (second year) jumped into action prepping the patient's right side with Betadine surgical solution as Renee prepared a chest tube kit. Cynthia looked at Jaime, not sure of what was about to happen as she grimaced in pain.

"My chest hurts!" Cynthia cried.

"They have to put a tube in your chest because your lung has collapsed and you aren't getting enough oxygen into your blood. They're going to numb the skin, but once they get past that, it's going to hurt. I'm sorry. The more you relax, the less painful it will be. Would it be okay if I stroke your forehead with my hand? Sometimes, that helps people relax. When we're in pain, our bodies tense. The more we tense, the more we hurt. The more we hurt, the more we tense. It's a vicious cycle. If you use your mind to tell your body to relax, it will hurt less."

"You're going to feel something like bee stings as I put the local anesthetic in," said Dr. Gutierrez. Cynthia winced as he stuck her several times, dispensing the numbing fluid. Jaime continued to stroke her head.

"What do you like to do when you're not working or hanging out in

11

trauma rooms?" Jaime asked his new best friend.

"I like to go dancing at Bali Pesters on The River Walk," Cynthia responded.

"Now would be a great time to go dancing. Just let your mind take you there while we do this procedure. It will just take a few minutes."

Jaime watched as the incision was made between Cynthia's ribs. Then the doctor, under Dr. Washington's supervision, indelicately placed his little finger in the hole to ensure he was above the patient's liver. "Iiiiieeee," Cynthia cried. Then he inserted the tube Renee handed him.

"Using a nineteen French" he said to the recorder over Cynthia's cries. Then Renee connected the other end of the tube to a vacuum pump and turned it on as Dr. Gutierrez sutured the tube into place.

"Iiiiieeeee!" cried Cynthia. "It hurts so bad. What's happening?"

"Take a few deep breaths and tell your body to relax," said the Chaplain. "When your lung begins to inflate you feel pain." Pause. "You handled that well. I know it hurt. Tell me the other feelings you were having when the car wrecked."

"It was so scary. Everything was in slow motion. I thought it would never stop!" She chuckled slightly, as to herself. "When I was hanging upside down, I thought about all the stuff I had to do at work. I feel so stupid. Then I got really scared again and wanted my mother to be there with me. This is going to be so hard on her and Dad. I'm afraid he'll have another heart attack."

"You're more scared for him and your mom than you are for yourself."

"Yes. I don't know if he can take it."

"Tell me more."

"He had a really bad heart attack in '03 and has been on disability since. Mom's had to take care of him, getting him back and forth to the doctor, rehab, and the drug store. She's had to do it all. I've tried to help, but I work and I'm dating someone. It's pretty serious and I want to spend as much time with him as I can." She paused, thoughtfully.

"And now you feel guilty for not helping Mom more and being with

12

them, more."

Cynthia nodded her head slowly as tears welled up and then ran down her cheeks.

"We're going to do a Foley, now chaplain," said the first year resident (Read: Intern). *By any name, a scared kid with no sense of what to do, other than what he's told*, thought Jaime. He made a mental note to spend some time with him after the resuscitation and to pray more for all the interns and residents.

"Cynthia, they're going to insert a Foley catheter. Do you know what that means?"

She nodded yes and then said, a bit embarrassed, "I had one when I was in the hospital for a really bad bladder infection." She paused as she was making her decision of what to say next. Then, in a whisper, "I got it after Frank and I...slept together the first time." She looked deeply into Jaime's eyes and said, "I thought it was God punishing me for being bad. The sisters and Father always said we should wait until marriage. Is that true?"

"What do you think?" asked Jaime.

31/1822 December 2005

Renee gave him an affirming look as one of the Licensed Vocational Nurses said, "Padre, the family is here."

"Thanks, Wimp. I'll be right there." William "Bill" Knoblauch was fifth-generation San Antonian. His forbearers immigrated from Germany in the late nineteenth century, as did many of their peers. He is a veteran of Operation Desert Shield/Storm where he served as a 91B, combat medic, with the Big Red One (First Infantry Division). He played defensive lineman for McArthur High School and made all state. He is only 5' 11" and was not recruited to play college ball, except for a couple of Division III universities. Therefore, he joined the army immediately after high school. He had not lost his bulked up, athletic build, or his way to the gym, hence the nickname, "Wimp."

"Cynthia, I'm going out to talk with your family. Is there anything you want me to tell them?"

"Just tell them I'm okay and not to worry. Especially tell my dad."

"You got it. I'll be back in just a few minutes," said Jaime, squeezing her shoulder, reassuringly. "Doc, anything you want me to tell her parents?"

Thaddeus thought for a moment and then said, "Tell them I'll be there in just a minute and that she's doing well. She has a compound fracture of the right femur, she's stable and oh, hell, I can break away. I'll just go with you, Chappie."

The two took off their goggles and latex gloves, then walked to the family room discussing the (Texas) A&M vs. FSU (Florida State) bowl game the night before. Thad tapped on the door of the family room before walking in. He did not wait for a response.

As Jaime walked in behind the doctor, he saw an overweight Hispanic man in his mid-sixties. He was wearing a pajama shirt, slacks, a brown, light jacket and house shoes. His face was twisted into a caricature of fear and helplessness. Next to him was a shorter, heavier Hispanic woman wearing a flower-print house dress, a sweater that didn't match and black slip-ons. If possible, she looked more worried than her husband. Standing behind both was a tall, slender, thirty something Hispanic male wearing a blue button down dress shirt, tan slacks, blue blazer and stylish loafers. His face showed concern, but not fear.

"Mr. and Mrs. Gonzalez?" Thad asked. The couple nodded simultaneously. "I'm Dr. Washington and I'm taking care of Cynthia." He then looked at the young man standing against the wall as if to say, who are you?

"I'm Francisco Perez, Cynthia's fiancé. Her parents called me as soon as they heard."

That was good enough for Thad to continue with HIPAA sensitive information. "She has a broken thigh and a collapsed lung. Her vitals are stable and we need to do a belly tap to determine if she has any internal bleeding, and CT scan to ensure she doesn't have any spinal complications. Right now, we don't anticipate any additional injuries, but we'll know more after the two tests. Do you have any questions?"

"When can we see her?" asked Mrs. Gonzalez.

"As soon as she gets back from CT," Thad responded, maybe forty-five minutes. The chaplain, here, will come and get you. I need to get back. I'll be back later." He left after shaking their hands.

"I'm Chaplain Jaime Martinez. They call us for all traumas, so please don't interpret my presence as a bad omen. I've been with Cynthia since she arrived. She's fully conscious and we have been talking about what she's been through to help minimize the emotional and spiritual impact of the accident. I'll get you in to see her as soon as I can. She told me to tell you that she's okay and to not worry—especially you, Dad." That broke some of the tension.

There was a knock on the door as a middle aged Caucasian woman with a clip board and a serious look on her face, walked in. She was the admissions clerk.

"Is there anything you would like me to tell her?" asked Jaime.

"Tell her we love her," said Mom.

"Tell her I'm okay," said Dad.

Jaime looked at Frank and he shook his head no.

"I'm going to see Cynthia. I'll be back here as soon as I can. Hello, Susan." The clerk nodded, solemnly.

31/1845 December 2005

"I just spoke to your parents and Francisco. Mom said to tell you they love you and Dad said he was okay. I think they are within-normal-limits."

"What did Frank say?" asked Cynthia.

"He's the strong, silent type, isn't he?" She nodded and Jaime added, "He looked worried and helpless. I'm guessing he doesn't do helpless

15

very well."

"No, he just gets angry."

"That's the only feeling our south Texas culture, Hispanic or *Gringo*, allows us guys to feel. If we're scared, we get angry. If we're hurting, we get angry. If we are helpless, we really get angry."

"That's Frank, alright. He's such a wonderful man, he just doesn't feel. Or if he does, he pushes it down until it goes away."

Cynthia was still naked from the waist up. The intern was doing a belly tap, an abdominal laparoscopy to determine if there was any internal bleeding, besides the little bit the chest tube caused. Fortunately, due to topical anesthetic, there was no pain involved in the procedure. She remained calm as she talked to Jaime, with intermittent spasms of uncontrolled shivering accompanied with goose bumps and, as Jaime noticed, hardened nipples.

"Belly tap is negative," announced the intern, looking relieved and duly proud of his own damned self. It is well known in the medical community, Hippocrates, father of occidental medicine, learned early in his career that telling a patient the procedure he was about to perform was his first, was not a confidence builder. Hence, Karl Sassmann, MD did not provide that information to Cynthia before stepping to the gurney with all the confidence he could and began.

Jaime began talking Cynthia through it, realizing that he was witnessing what The Reverend Doctor Charles McRae, BCC, LPC called, "The duck phenomenon," i.e., the intern was gently gliding across the pond while paddling like hell below the surface. When the procedure was over, Thaddeus T. Washington, MD gave the intern a "Good job, Doctor." Jaime noticed a bit of justified feather puffing going on with Dr. Sassmann.

As soon as the procedure was finished, Jaime pulled the green hospital sheet up to Cynthia's neck. She looked up at him and said softly, "Thank you."

"Okay, let's get her to CT," directed Dr. Washington. The entire medical team descended on the gurney and Cynthia as preparation was

16

made to transport her. Jaime began explaining what was about to happen and that he would bring her family in to see her when she got back to the Emergency Department.

"Is there anything I can do to be useful to you before you go to CT?" asked Jaime.

"Just keep me in your prayers," she said with a faint smile.

"Would you like to have one now?" She looked around the room at the staff busily preparing for the short ride to the scanner. They seemed to be paying no attention to her or the chaplain. She nodded.

"Creator God, we don't understand why this happened today. But we do know that you are still in control and that your love surrounds Cynthia and her family as they go through this difficult situation. We give you thanks for the staff who have dedicated their lives to your healing ministry and the men and women who have had the insight to build great hospitals like Mercy Methodist to your glory and for the care of your children. Hold Cynthia close and remind her of how much you love her. 'When she is frightened, give her courage, when she is weak, give her strength and when she is anxious give her peace.' In the name of the Father, and of the Son, and of the Holy Spirit, Amen." Jaime made the sign of the Cross over Cynthia as he ended the prayer. She silently crossed herself. A tear ran down the side of Cynthia's face as Renee announced they were ready to go.

Jaime watched the CNA (Certified Nurses' Aid) and CT tech push the gurney out of Trauma Room B. "Great job, everyone," announced Dr. Washington. "Chalk one up for the good guys."

There was a collective sigh of relief as people began to filter out of the room. The recorder was the last to leave as two custodians came in to clean. "You guys always get the dirty work, don't you?"

"*Sí, Capellán, no fuera por eso, no tendria trabajo.*"

"Indeed it is Juan. As long as there's trauma, you'll have a job!" said Jaime, laughing. He was starting to decompress. "¿*Cómo están sus esposa y niños?*"

"My wife is still working too hard, but at least she is young. She misses her *madre* in Mexico. The boys are growing strong *y mi hija es más bonita cada día!"*

"¿Cuántos años tiene, ella?" asked Jaime.

"Cuatro años, capellán. She can already speak English and say her ABCs."

"Ella está muy inteligente," he paused, *"Y bonita.* How do four year olds get so smart so fast?"

"Mi esposa." Juan replied with a smile.

"No doubt she gets her beauty from her mother as well," laughed Jaime.

"Sí, cierto."

"Of course it's true, *el capellán dijo!"*

"Sí padre. Sí."

"Hello, I'm Jaime Martinez. I'm one of the chaplains here," he said to the other custodian.

"I'm Laticia Greene. You sure do speak that Mexican stuff good."

"Thank you, Ms. Greene."

"Laticia, please."

"Thank you, Laticia. Have you been working here long? I don't think I've seen you before."

"I was working at Central Methodist, but we moved from the east side to over here, so I transferred. The schools are better and this is closer. It's only one bus ride away, I don't have to transfer. It only takes thirty minutes to get to or from work."

"That's good. Tell me about your children," said Jaime.

"Michela is thirteen and Leshan is ten. She's a cheerleader at Jackson Middle School. Leshan just loves his Game Boy and plays it all the time."

"They both sound pretty normal to me. Does Michela do that thing of walking through the house silently making the hand signals of the cheers?" asked Jaime, smiling.

"You know she does. The child does cheers in her sleep!"

"I know that deal. It was good to meet you, Laticia. I have to go visit with the family of our trauma patient. Good to have you on the

18

team."

"You have a blessed day, Chaplain."

31/1900 December 2005

Jaime rapped on the door of the family room as he walked in. Mr. and Mrs. Gonzalez were sitting next to each other on the love seat. Francisco was not in the room. "I just saw Cynthia and she is doing fine. They are getting ready to bring her back from CT. How are you?"

"We're okay. When will we get to see her?" Mrs. Gonzalez asked, as she dabbed at her eyes with a tissue.

"Soon. I'm going off shift now, and Chaplain Womac will be down to see you in just a few minutes, if we don't have another crisis for a while. She will take you in to see Cynthia as soon as possible, after she gets back to the ED. Is there anything I can do to be useful to you, before I leave?" They both shook their heads. "Here is my card and I will keep all of you in my prayers. Please tell Francisco I said good-bye."

"We will," Mrs. Gonzalez said. "He's outside talking on his cell phone. He is on it, constantly. He's a good man and we are happy for him and Cynthia, but he is just so busy all the time. And now, she tells us that he has been offered a job in Seattle. Cynthia is our youngest, our baby. We don't want them to move."

"Of course not," said Jaime as he glanced at his watch and then chided himself for doing it. I know that is a big concern for both of you. Perhaps we can talk about it when I see you Tuesday. *Hasta luego,*" said Jaime. He shook hands with both and left.

Way to go, pendejo. That was just frikin' brilliant, looking at your watch in there. Very pastoral. Very pastoral, indeed. Jaime walked past the elevators and took the stairs to the fourth floor to get rid of his self anger. He was still pissed when he took the elevator to the twelfth floor, but his legs were complaining about the abuse. It had been a hard shift. All he wanted now

19

was to go home, get a shower and then some sleep.

31/1915 December 2005

Jaime sat at the desk in the Clinical Chaplaincy office finishing the "Duty Log" entries for his shift. Memory was not coming to him easily. He was exhausted. He couldn't get Cynthia and her family out of his mind. She should do well. He knew he would follow-up with her when he worked the day after tomorrow. Still, he had an uneasy feeling about her.

He also had a king sized dollop of guilt. That's roughly equivalent to five bleams, a unit of measure for emotions as defined by The Reverend Doctor Charles McRae, BCC, LPC (Board Certified Chaplain and Licensed Professional Counselor), Vice President for Pastoral Care, Mercy Methodist Health System. Jaime couldn't quit thinking of the image of Cynthia's beautiful, naked body. The intrusive thoughts were frustrating and scary. "Am I going nuts?" he thought to himself. "What would Sister say? Do I have to tell her? I don't want to share this in IPR (Interpersonal Relationship Group, a part of his residency training)."

"That's a deep thought," said Sandy Womac, M. Div., another Chaplain resident. She was Jaime's relief and had the 7:00p to 7:00a shift. She would welcome the New Year amongst death, life, and broken bodies.

Sandy was twenty-seven years old, five foot even, petite, blue eyed blond with a sweet, heart shaped face and long, straight hair. Most men would also suggest, with the highest possible respect, that she was built like a brick outhouse.

Her looks were often distracting to male colleagues and a disadvantage in establishing her professional credibility. One reason she opted for clinical chaplaincy was that the South Texas congregations of her denomination (Presbyterian) had trouble taking her seriously as their pastor. She had also been the recipient of jealousy motivated criticism from female colleagues and/or parishioners.

Sandy's words had the effect of a cannon firing. Jaime actually jumped. He gave himself a moment to settle and focus. "Yeah, I had a tough shift. Got a young woman in tonight that I just don't feel good about. Not sure why. She's a rollover MVA with a fractured femur, broken ribs and pnuemo. Should do well. Nice family and good looking fiancé. Would you mind looking in on them? Her name is Cynthia Gonzalez. She should be back from CT by now and the family is anxious to see her. A single young woman such as yourself might enjoy meeting her fiancé," added Jaime with a devilish grin. Sandy just rolled her eyes and gave him one of those "Is that all you think about?" looks.

"Sounds tough." You know what Sister Joyce says, "Trust your gut."

"Yeah, that's what scares me. Sure hope I'm wrong." He continued his "report" until he had warned her of all the landmines waiting for her.

"Sorry I was late getting up here. I got snagged by the Nursing Night Supervisor. There's a family in MICU who's raising cane and threatening a lawsuit. Wants me to see them."

"Yeah, the Dietermanns. If you can't control Momma dying," he started, "You can always chew out the staff or sue," Sandy finished for him. "See, I was awake when Dr. McRae was teaching that class."

"I would appreciate it if you saw the Gonzalez family first, and get them in to see Cynthia." Jaime paused, thoughtfully. "Well, I'm out of here. I'm going to enjoy the rest of the holiday as much as possible. Hope you have a good night."

"Yeah, like that's going to happen on New Year's Eve," said Sandy. "Can you speak 'Drunk'? I need a crash course." As Jaime walked out of the office, Sandy slid into the chair he had just vacated and began to read the log. She took a deep breath as she steeled herself for the next twelve hours. "Dear God, please don't let me screw up," she prayed as she headed for the door.

CHAPTER 2

31/2359 December 2005

"Five, four, three, two, one, Happy New Year!" Chaplain Charles S. McRae, D. Min., BCC, LPC chastely kissed his wife of twenty-four years and took a sip of his champagne. He abhorred formal fund raisers. The Crystal Ball was an annual New Year's Eve event benefiting Mercy Methodist Hospital, a not-for-profit, faith-based, 625 bed tertiary facility. When it became the flagship for the Mercy Methodist Health System (MMHS) almost a year earlier, the decision was made to have one last event, benefiting the charitable organizations MMH had supported for many years.

Charles had been the Vice President for Pastoral Care for five years. He had been in hospital ministry for nineteen years and had been an ordained "Elder in full connection," with the Southwest Texas Conference (SWTC) of the United Methodist Church, for twenty-five years.

The aristocracy of San Antonio was present. Charles thought to himself, *if they gave what they paid for their clothes instead of the chump change $150 per plate, they would raise a hell of a lot more money, and they could stay home on New Year's Eve like I wanted to do.*

The chandeliered grand ballroom of the St. Timothy Hotel in downtown San Antonio was on the Texas State Historical Registry. It had been the second such facility established after the Battle of Texas Independence by the gallant Texians, as they called themselves then, under the command of General Sam Houston at San Jacinto, 21 April 1836. It had been the site of many important events during the nine years of the Republic and later, the State of Texas. The red brick façade was a familiar landmark.

Charles whispered into his wife's ear that after the next dance, he wanted to go to their hotel room, watch a few fireworks and then, perhaps, make some of their own. She grinned coyly and began to walk toward the door. Charles didn't mind skipping the dance.

They said good night to Bill Groene, FACHE (Fellow of the American College of Healthcare Executives), Chief Executive Officer of Mercy Methodist Health System, and his wife, Tammy. Both were native Texans and had the accents to prove it. Charles and Bill were the same age and had graduated from rival schools. Bill was a University of Texas grad while Charles was from Texas A&M. They enjoyed teasing each other about it. Charles was one of Bill's eight direct reports.

01/0235 January 2006

Chaplain (Resident) Sandy Womac's pager buzzed. She excused herself and walked away from the bedside of a patient she was visiting while "rounding" in SICU. "Imminent death on 5W. Pls report asap," the creeper read across the screen on top of the pager. Sandy wasn't sure who was dying, but the odds were good she would know the patient and family. The oncology unit was one of her responsibilities. She began walking to the elevators. *I'm too tired to be doing stairs*, she thought to herself as she pushed the up button.

"Oh, Chaplain, thanks for coming so quickly. Mr. Robinson is just about to transition," said the charge nurse when Sandy walked up to the station desk. "He's in sixteen," she added. Sandy just nodded as she began walking toward the patient room. She began to steel herself for what was about to happen.

Can't believe he is going this fast. He was just diagnosed in July. I thought he would have at least a year. What a shame. The young chaplain's internal solilo-

23

quy continued as she reluctantly walked down the hallway.

Tom Robinson had been Sandy's first patient to be diagnosed with life threatening (Read: Terminal) cancer. The primary site was the left lung, but it had already metastasized when he was diagnosed. Stage four. Sandy had been called in by the attending physician to be present for the meeting with the Robinsons to tell them the bad news. He was "concerned" the patient and/or his wife would "get emotional" when he told them. As a scientist and sometime researcher, feelings were an inconvenience at best and usually downright unpleasant—especially if he was the one having them, which, of course, he would never admit to himself or others.

Sandy had been very helpful, at least to him, even though the Robinsons accepted the news with grace and dignity. The doctor left as soon as he could after he delivered the diagnosis and asked if they had any questions, looking much more uncomfortable than the patient or his wife. The truth be told, the young chaplain wasn't feeling all that good herself, but she managed a calm presence and began to work for an emotional release from the Robinsons, whom she had met five minutes before. "I'm sure that was not what either of you were expecting. Please tell me the feelings you are experiencing right now," said Sandy. *I'm about to hurl, and I'm asking them how* **they** *feel?* God give me strength, she prayed and begged at the same time.

"Well, I've always wondered how the Good Lord was going to take me, and now I know," was all Tom said. He stood, turned to his wife and said quite gently, "Come, Mother, I guess we have a lot to do. Let's go home." With that, they thanked the shocked chaplain (resident) and walked out of the room.

Sandy collapsed into a chair to process what had just happened. She had never seen anyone respond to bad news like that before, nor has she since. *That was amazing. I don't think I have ever seen anyone with that kind of faith. Or maybe it's just denial, like Sister Joyce told us to watch for. Oh, fecal matter, I should have walked them out of the hospital.*

Over the next five plus months Sandy had become quite close to the Robinsons. She learned he was the senior deacon in their Southern

Baptist Church and that he had accepted Jesus Christ as his Lord and Savior when he was nine years old at a tent revival his church sponsored. "I've never regretted that decision," he said to her on several occasions as she walked through the valley with him and his wife. Now, it was almost over and she felt sad—very, very sad.

She tapped on the door of the darkened room as she walked in. Melissa Robinson sat next to Tom's bed, holding his hand. When she saw Sandy, she smiled and a tear ran down her cheek. "I'm so glad it's you. We were just talking about how we hoped you were in the hospital tonight. Your being here will mean a lot to Tom. Thank you."

Sandy was temporarily speechless. She reached out and hugged Melissa as the two cried softly together. Sandy then walked to the side of the bed opposite where the wife had been sitting. Tom was breathing in shallow rapid breaths with his mouth open, making an almost perfect O shape. She took his other hand, leaned close to his ear and said softly, "Tom, its Chaplain Sandy. I just wanted to be with you and Melissa. Is that okay?"

Slowly, his eyes opened and he nodded his head, slightly. Sandy thought she saw a small smile at one corner of his mouth. "Thank you," he said with some effort, barely audible.

My God, he's lost so much weight and he looks ten years older than when I saw him a month ago, she thought to herself as she made a mental note of everything in the room and most especially his condition. When she first met him, he was 6' 2" and weighed 230 pounds. He seemed quite robust, was full of life and had twinkling blue eyes. *Now this. Dear God, what are you thinking?*

Sandy placed her other hand on his shoulder and asked, "Would you like to have a word of prayer?" She saw the smile increase ever so slightly and without opening his eyes, he nodded. She took Melissa's hand as she continued to gently press on his shoulder with the other one.

"Holy and loving God, thank you for Tom and Melissa and what they mean to your kingdom. Thank you for the years of service and ministry they have provided through your Church and for all the lives they have

25

touched in living the Good News of Jesus Christ. I thank you that you have allowed me to know these, your dear children, and for all the blessings they have given me as we have walked this journey together. We commend our brother, Tom, and ask that you receive him unto yourself as he transitions into the Church Triumphant. Hold him close and remind him of the love of those of us who mourn his passing.

"We pray you will be with Melissa, the children and their children. Provide for them the Holy Comforter in their time of loss and walk with them as they rejoice in the love they have received from Tom. Remind them of his wisdom and his faith, and grant them your peace, even that peace which surpasses all human understanding. These things we pray, in the name of the risen Christ. Amen."

As Sandy opened her eyes and wiped her tears away, she saw one run down Tom's cheek. "Tom, I want you to know that I'm going to look after Melissa and the family and I want you to know they are going to be okay. They have wonderful faith and wonderful support groups to get them through this hard time. You don't have to worry about them. They are of your stock." She then said the twenty-third Psalm. Four minutes later, Tom Robinson breathed his last.

Melissa stood, leaned over the bed railing and gently kissed her husband of forty-seven years. She looked at Sandy and said, "What now?"

01/0830 January 2006

Charles joined MMHS one month after the partnership between Mercy Methodist Hospital and Health Source, Inc. HSI, the third largest owner of health care facilities in the nation, owned four smaller hospitals in San Antonio. He fell into the job of a lifetime, getting to create what became the only Level I Pastoral Care Service in the state and all of HSI.

There were seven other qualified applicants for the position, and he was the one selected. His joy was eclipsed only by his feelings of unworthiness and fear. "It was sort of like a dog chasing a car," he told a friend. "I didn't know what to do with it once I caught it!"

His starting salary was more money than he ever expected to make in his life. He was in "The Show," and he just kept wondering what Marc and Martha McRae's baby boy was doing here. His Bishop told Charles he would be appointed to the Vice President position, and that the "Wall Street Journal" and the National Health Care Community would be watching to see what happened with the partnership of a not-for-profit entity, i.e., the foundation established by the partnership, and a for-profit, publicly traded company, HSI.

One of the nine agreements in the founding document for MMHS was that there would be a "System-wide department of Pastoral Care and the chief of that department would be appointed by the United Methodist Bishop of the San Antonio Area."

HSI never knew what they agreed to; Charles would remind himself, and his Directors, on a regular basis. He never failed to be amused by the agreement. "I don't think they could spell PCS until a couple of years after we got started," Charles had said on a few occasions. "I think they just decided that a few thousand dollars was worth appeasing the Board of Trustees of Mercy Methodist Hospital. They were eager to be in partnership with MMH, since it was the market leader in San Antonio. It had thirty-four percent of the market share when the partnership was formed. They had no idea what the Board had in mind."

Charles always delighted in telling the story of his one and only attendance at the monthly Board of Governors meeting. The brilliance of that ten member group, five from the board of directors of Mercy Methodist Ministries, the not-for-profit foundation established by the partnership in place of the MMH Board of Trustees, and five from HSI was that there were only two votes. All decisions were made by consensus.

He was there to present his first ever budget. He had been with MMHS for only three months. He and Bill had spent several hours massaging the presentation to optimize its acceptance without major modification (Read: Reduction). A surprise to most, especially Charles, was that

27

Don Thompson, FACHE, Chief Operating Officer of Healthcare Source, Inc. was present.

He asked several pointed questions about how serious Charles and the other chaplains were about actually achieving the projected revenue and cost avoidance. Several of the "locals" also had some tough questions, but in the end, the $1.3 million budget passed as presented.

"When Don Thompson saw that figure the first time in the meeting, he almost swallowed his snuff," Charles would say in subsequent retellings of the event. It always got a polite chuckle from those listening.

Charles was remembering those events as he sipped his coffee while, multitasking by enjoying the natural beauty of his wife as she brushed her hair. The sun was shining brightly through the glass doors with shear drapes leading to the balcony of their hotel room. Her gown had become transparent and he drank in her nakedness. He began to remember their lovemaking much earlier that morning. Life was good, and he knew he was blessed among men.

Beth turned from the mirror and read his mind as he smiled lovingly at her. She blushed. After a moment, she walked to where Charles was sitting with his feet propped on the desk, slipped the spaghetti straps off her shoulders and let the gown fall to the floor. She took his hand and led him to the bed. No words were spoken.

01/1027 January 2006

Charles awoke to the always pleasant sound of Beth singing in the shower. He lay in the bed absorbing the last few hours. The thought of the upcoming Budget Review Committee intruded on his revelry. He began to think of the budget presentation he had to make on Friday, with the usual questions of justification for this or that program. He had a perpetual offer to Bill Groene that if Bill would just give him a sound beating and approve the budget as submitted, he would prefer that to the committee's grilling. That never happened.

The committee was composed of Bill Groene, CEO, the Chair of the Board of Governors, the Chief Nursing Executive, the System Chief Financial Officer, the System Executive Vice President (a recovering CFO), the System Development Vice President (Read: Chief negotiator for contracts with managed care companies), the two CEOs of the hospital groups and the System Comptroller.

It would be a tough sale to get approval for the Clinical Pastoral Education program increase. He was proposing adding two Supervisors-In-Training (SITs) to increase the number of summer interns/seminarians and residents. Convincing bean counters of the efficacy of more training opportunities for potential clinical chaplains and quantifying the benefits of same was a monumental challenge.

No small part of the problem was that Charles' personality type, i.e., how he viewed the world, was antithetical to those on the committee. Each one just wanted the facts, as defined by lots of numbers. That which they could not quantify, they did not value.

The really good news was that they were all people of faith and were active, to varying degrees, in their religious community. Theologically, they ran the gamut. One of Charles' ongoing challenges, and that of his staff, was educating them and everyone else in health care, as to what a clinically trained chaplain was, what their "value addedness" was to the operation and how they differed from the Reverend Billy Bob of the Left Handed Church of Jesus Christ of What's Happening Now when he was visiting one of his parishioners. Too often, Charles felt a major disconnect with his corporate colleagues. Conversely, what little he understood about the inner working of the System was lost on the chaplain clinicians. His professional life was a constant netherworld between his calling to and the context of his ministry.

He was so deep in thought that Beth's announcement that she was ready to go to brunch, and then check out, caused him to actually jump. His mind turned quickly from work to pleasure. "Why don't we stay another day and play like we don't have to go to work tomorrow?" asked

29

Charles, innocently. Beth just rolled her eyes as she smiled her "you're such a little boy, sometimes" smile. Charles threw on some clothes and they headed downstairs for the brunch. "By the way," Beth said with a twinkle in her eye, "you're too old to spend another day making love."

"Ouch! Even if it's true, you don't have to remind me," he said grabbing her bottom as she walked on to the elevator. She blushed and then snuggled next to him as the doors closed.

01/1145 January 2006

"I need your help on something," Charles said to Beth as they were enjoying their post brunch coffee. She looked at him seriously and nodded in a "tell me more" kind of way. "The budget meeting is this Friday. I'm asking for $105,000 to create two SIT positions for the Clinical Pastoral Education program. That's a four per cent increase before we add the raises and inflation factor. All together it's going to be a seven per cent increase. That's pretty steep *fer der Erbsenzalers* (Bean Counters)."

"What's the guidance from the bean counters this year?"

"Four percent."

"How much did you offset the operating expenses with the cost avoidance and revenue?" she asked.

"Twenty-seven percent. We sold a twenty hour per week chaplain to Bulverde County Regional Medical Center in Uvalde and a full timer to MacAfee Memorial in Jourdanton. Johnny Jones has been extremely helpful with getting me in to see the CEOs of the rural hospitals. He's really a prince of a guy."

Johnny retired from the Army as a Medical Service Corp full Colonel (0-6) and then was CEO of the county hospital in San Marcos for fifteen years. When he retired from that, Bill Groene money-whipped him into coming on staff, part-time, as the VP for Rural Outreach. Bill always introduced him as the Dean of Rural Healthcare in South Texas. Bill and

Charles shared the opinion, along with many others, that they just don't come any finer than Johnny Jones, FACHE.

Charles had spent several delightful days traveling with Johnny to the towns in the seventeen county catchment area of MMHS, meeting CEOs and their senior leadership teams to build relationships between them and MMHS. Johnny even sweetened the pot of the hospital board of directors signing one of four management contracts with MMHS by making benefit of same a free Pastoral Care needs assessment and recommended strategy to achieve the Hospitals' goals in that area by the VP of Pastoral Care, MMHS. It was often the tie breaker in deciding to go with Mercy Methodist. Charles always looked forward to being with Johnny.

"I hope you don't use such crass phrasing as 'selling chaplains to other hospitals' when you're in public, dear. It just doesn't sound quite right," Beth gently chided.

"You know what I mean and no I don't talk like that around those who are not so enamored with me, as you."

"Says who?" she quickly responded. She had a twinkle in her eye when she said it and Charles felt very loved.

"So how do I pitch the budget?"

"I think the key is to show them the benefits in dollars and cents of having an SIT program and the way you can increase good will and out migration, isn't that what you call getting patient referrals with the rurals and the larger hospitals in Laredo, Del Rio, Victoria, New Braunfelds and San Marcos? It's important for them to see the connection between the SITs and the training of clergy and chaplains in South Texas. You are going to be using them to increase the extension program, right?"

"Right. I'm just not sure how to quantify that connection. I can't say we'll get an 'x' percent increase in out migration just because they had some of their people, especially local pastors who voluntarily pull on-call for them, in CPE with us."

"No, I guess you can't, but you can quantify how many of the pastors you have already trained. Joyce can do a quick telephone survey with her former students and see what kind of anecdotal information she can get. Two or three good sound bites should help the cause. You can call a couple of the CEOs where an under trained chaplain did CPE with you and how their performance improved. That should be a good selling point, CEO to CEO."

"I like that. Everything else is pretty much what they have told us we have to do by way of increasing the budgets. Maybe I should quote a few stats from ACPE (the Association for Clinical Pastoral Education). As the cognate group for CPE, they should have some data to support the cause." Charles then let his mind wander to the meeting and what types of data would be most convincing. "It sure would make it a lot easier if they all just thought like me and understood the importance of CPE!"

"Fortunately, they don't think like you, or the System would be in deep trouble, fiscally. You just have to think like a Chief Financial Officer for a while until you can figure out what would make sense to them. What is it your mentor, Dorothy Satten, calls that, role reversal?"

"Yeah, that's the term. Thanks, Honey, for your help. This has been useful." Beth felt a special closeness with Charles. Then she looked at her watch. "We need to check out. It's almost one."

"*Always the pragmatist,*" thought Charles. "*God, I do love that woman.*" He gave a short prayer of thanksgiving for his good fortune in being married to Beth. He followed her out of the restaurant to the bank of elevators. She took his hand as he moved beside her and his heart leapt. He also felt very relieved about the budget review meeting on Friday.

CHAPTER 3

01/0720 January 2006

CH (LTC, USAF-RET) Thomas A. Wilson, M. Div, MS, LMFT Chaplain Resident, closed the chaplains' log, took a deep breath and said a quick prayer. Sandy Womac got hammered the previous shift; three deaths, two code blues and three traumas, accounting for one of the deaths. He pushed himself out of the chair and headed for the ER to see what was happening. He had hoped to watch some of the NFL games, but didn't hold out much hope for that scenario. The good news was that the college bowl games would be postponed until tomorrow, when he would be off, because New Year's Day fell on a Sunday.

The ER was slow and he took the time to talk with the two EMTs who had brought in the early morning trauma case. They had just completed making ready the ambulance for its next run and it was obvious to Tom, they were really hurting.

The patient was a four year old Caucasian girl whose clothes caught fire when a bottle rocket struck her as her brother and step father were discharging fire works on New Year's Eve. She had sustained burns over seventy-five percent of her body. Most were full thickness, or third degree as the laity called them. The rookie EMT had never seen a burn patient before last night. It was particularly difficult in that it was a "Pedi burn", i.e., a child.

Tom listened as he took them through an informal debriefing, sometimes called a defusing. They told him, with his guidance, what they had done at the scene and on their way to the ER. Then he said, "Tell me what thoughts you were having as this went on." The senior EMT talked about trying to remember the protocols for burns. He thought about how young Diane is and the massive injuries on her small body. The rookie talked about how scared he was that he might screw up. It also really "bothered" him to start the IV on her and the pain he caused by moving her. "I just felt terrible about hurting her, but I knew I had to. I hope I never have to do that again." Tears began to form in his eyes as he turned away. Tom put his hand on the young man's shoulder and gently said, "It's okay to cry."

The dam broke and the rookie cried hard tears for a minute or so. Then he wiped his eyes with the back of his hand and sheepishly looked at Tom and his partner. "Thanks, Padre. I feel better."

"Tell me what feelings you had, Jose'." The lead EMT cleared his throat and said, "I just wish we could have gotten there quicker. We got the call about 2233 and the traffic was unusually heavy. Maybe we could have done more. Those dumb SOBs wouldn't get out of the way. We were Code three (lights and sirens) and used all the extra sounds we had available and they just wouldn't let us through."

"Sounds like you're pretty angry," said Tom.

"Stupid people just piss me off", said Jose'.

"You must spend a lot of time being angry when you're driving," said Tom with a smile.

Jose' and the rookie both laughed. "Tell me, what was the worst part for you?"

"She just kept screaming. No matter what we did, she just kept screaming. I felt so helpless. Gave me the willies," said Jose'.

"When I took hold of her arm to start the IV, some of her skin just came off in my hand. It was gross. I almost hurled. They didn't teach us what to do when that happens," confessed the rookie.

"Sounds like this is one you're not going to forget for awhile," mused Tom.

"I don't think I'll ever forget those screams," said Jose'. "I can still hear her. Every time I close my eyes I see her burned body," he said.

"Yeah, me too," said the rookie. "I can't quit thinking about it. I wish I could."

"Sounds like you're both totally normal to me," said the Chaplain. "You're probably going to be having intrusive thoughts for a few days and may have some bad dreams or trouble sleeping. You're already starting to second guess what you could have done better, or at least differently. That's all normal." Tom let them absorb what he had just said and then began again, "I just happen to have a brochure for each of you on the signs of PTS (Post Traumatic Stress). It's the normal reaction of the mind, body and soul to a traumatic event."

"Yeah, I was praying the whole way here and at the same time wondering why God would let this happen. It was very confusing," said the rookie.

"You're angry with God."

"No, I'm not angry with him. I just don't understand why he would do this. I mean, what could she have possibly done to deserve this? It just doesn't seem fair. Why wasn't her dumbass stepfather hurt? He's the one who should have been watching her. What a jerk. Fireworks with a four year old. It just doesn't make sense."

"Tell me more," Tom said, softly.

"Hell, I don't know, Chaplain. It's just so damned unfair."

"No one was watching out for her?"

"Yeah, I thought God was supposed to protect children."

"He did a pretty piss poor job with this one, didn't he?"

"Yeah, I guess I am pretty mad at God. This kind of shit just shouldn't be happening. I can understand it if someone does something stupid and gets hurt, but this just makes no sense."

"Tell me what you'd like to tell God, right now, if you could say anything you wanted with no repercussions, no consequences."

"I'd tell him he really fu…, screwed up. He should have been protecting her and not let her get burned like that. I mean, if she lives, her life

35

is really going to be messed up."

"Yes it is," agreed Tom.

"It's just not fair," he said in a whisper as new tears ran down his face. "It's just not fair, at all."

"No it's not."

"Padre, why does God let this kind of stuff happen?"

"I don't know," said Tom.

The rookie looked at him with surprise. He paused and then said thoughtfully, "I guess no one does."

"No. No one knows. And if anyone ever tells you they do, then duck. You don't want to get hit with the bovine organic mulch they're slingin'."

The rookie and Jose' chuckled softly, as the tension began to dissipate. "I've seen a lot of burn victims in my day, but the kids are always the toughest," said Jose'.

"That's been my experience," agreed Tom. "You just never get used to it. If we ever do, we're way past burnout and need to get out of the biz."

"Got that right, Chaplain," agreed Jose'. "These are the cases that cause me to question whether or not I want to keep doing this. There's got to be a better way to make a living."

"I've been there—many times. I guess we're both pretty normal. Tell me something else, where do you guys see hope in all of this?" asked Tom.

The rookie blurted, "I hit the vein on the first stick. I couldn't see squat and I just hit it. That helped me to relax, or at least be less scared. I've only been on the truck for four months and this is by far the worst case I've handled. I guess we must have done something right if she was alive when we got here."

"We were able to help the mom by telling her what we were doing and letting her ride in the back of the truck with her. She got the little girl to quit screaming and not be so afraid. That helped a lot," added Jose'.

"I wonder if we could look at it from a new perspective?" asked

Tom. "You were able to save her life and help the mom, too."

"Yeah I guess we did," said Jose'.

The rookie just nodded his head as he let the moment sink in. "Awesome," was all he said.

"Here's my card with my pager number on it. Give me a shout next time you make a run here and I'll buy the coffee. Deal?"

"Deal," they said in unison.

"I'm going up to check on her when I finish my rounds. I'll tell her you said hi. See you guys around the campus."

Wow, that debriefing stuff really works. They weren't half as stressed when we finished and it only took fifteen minutes. I thought it was a load of crap when Sister Joyce made us go to that two day training on Critical Incident Stress Management. Glad I did, now. He made his rounds through the ICUs. Nothing was happening that wouldn't wait. *Maybe, I'll have an easy day,* he thought to himself.

01/0940 January 2006

Chaplain (Resident) Tom Wilson, M. Div., MS., LMFT went to the burn unit to see how Diane was, knowing she wouldn't be good. He checked in with the charge nurse to let her know he was there and if any of the staff or other patients needed his attention. This was not his favorite place. He had serious intrusive thoughts of the burned soldiers he had prayed over in Iraq, when he walked onto the unit.

He had done a twelve month tour with an Army hospital unit in 2005. As soon as he saw her, he immediately remembered a five-year-old Iraqi girl who had died in his arms following a car bombing near her home in Baghdad. Seeing Diane brought it all back. He was having difficulty maintaining his Professional Distance, *Whatever the hell that is,* he thought to himself as he was putting on the gown, mask, cap, booties and sterile gloves necessary to go into the glass walled cubicle.

Thankfully, she was sleeping, (Read: Heavily sedated). A woman sat next to the bed with her hand on the girl's left shoulder, one of the few parts of her body not burned. Diane Worster had just gone through her first debriding. It was usually an excruciatingly painful process in which the nonviable tissue was removed with hemostats. The wounds were then scrubbed with sponges saturated with Betadine (antiseptic) solution. Then the injuries were covered in a white cream named Silvadene. The overwhelming consensus of the burn patients is that, as one sergeant put it, "It burns like hell, Sir!"

Silvadene was invented at the Institute of Surgical Research, better known as the Army Burn Unit. The Unit was established shortly after World War II with the mission of researching better treatment protocols for gunshot wounds and burns—both common injuries in combat. Eventually the former research was discontinued and it became the "grand daddy" of all burn units, worldwide. Until the mid 1990s the senior physicians of any burn unit had spent time training at the ISR.

It was a tenant unit of Brooke Army Medical Center, Fort Sam Houston, TX in San Antonio. BAMC is the trauma research center of the Army and Department of Defense. The acuity, i.e., seriousness of injury, of trauma patients, including burns, is greater at BAMC than any other hospital in DOD. In 1996, the Medical Center went from the configuration of being located in fifty-nine buildings on Fort Sam Houston, Texas to three facilities on a new campus contingent to the Post. It was a state of the art hospital with inpatient and outpatient facilities, a Level I (the highest) Trauma Center and the inpatient portion of the ISR.

Diane was intubated and the respirator was breathing for her. *Obviously, she had inhalation damage to her throat, larynx, bronchi and possibly her lungs*, thought Chaplain Wilson. The good news was, the physicians could give enough pain medication to provide her relief. Also, she was chemically paralyzed so as to not fight the breathing machine. The other small blessing in all this was that with so much of the burn being full thickness, the nerve endings in the skin were destroyed and, therefore, sent no pain impulses to the brain.

Tom noticed that the Docs had performed two escharotomies on the small child. One ran from her right wrist to the shoulder of the same arm on both the anterior and posterior, front and back sides. The other two incisions ran from her right ankle to her groin, anterior and posterior. The ones on her arm were about three-eighths of an inch wide and the ones on her leg were just slightly larger. At the vortex of each, Tom could see pink, healthy tissue. That was a good sign.

When the incisions were made, they were the width of the scalpel blade. They expanded as extracellar fluid accumulated to cause edema, swelling. Tom knew this is the standard procedure when a burn is full circumference of a limb and/or the torso. On the surface was a leathery, non-viable tissue called eschar. It was the six layers of skin that had been burned all the way through. In a few parts of Diane's body, the injury continued through the fascia, the white membrane covering the muscle, and into it.

Eschar is non-elastic. Therefore, as the body part swells, the veins and arteries are pinched shut, depriving the extremities of blood and oxygen. If the torso is a full circumference burn, the patient experiences suffocating pressure and, like a cave-in victim, cannot expand the chest cavity to force air into the lungs. The procedure to correct this is done without anesthetic because there is no sensation of pain in the dead tissue.

Diane was lying on her back, her arms at a ninety degree angle to her body and held above her chest by a web like gauze that hung from two IV poles attached to the bed. The sling worked like Chinese finger cuffs, the woven straw toys played with by children the world over. The more the child pulls their fingers apart, the more the cuff tightens. If they push their fingertips toward each other, the cuff "relaxes" its hold and the fingers are free.

The burned parts of her body were covered in the white cream and she had a small piece of gauze covering her genitalia. She was otherwise, completely naked. Her face was burned as was the right side of her scalp. Her head had been shaved to prevent a misplaced hair causing an infection.

Tom knew it was too early to know if she had partial or full thickness injury to her face. He had learned from his first six month rotation, spent on the step down unit for Burn ICU, that it takes about seventy-two hours for a burn to "mature." What initially appears to be partial thickness, second degree, may become full thickness.

If it were the former, as he prayed it would be, the scarring would be minimal or, perhaps, non-existent. If it was the latter, skin grafts would have to be applied and the scarring could be severe. *God, what the fuck are you thinking that your precious child would be injured in this way?* His eyes watered and he took a moment to prepare himself for what was next.

Tom moved to the woman dressed in the same sterile coverings as he, introduced himself and was not surprised to hear that she was Diane's mom, Tamara Collins. "How long have you been in here?" Tom asked the anxious mom.

"About an hour and a half. They let me in as soon as they were through cleaning her up." *Read: Debridement* Tom thought to himself, but refrained from sharing. "Thank God they were able to knock her out for that. I hate to think what that would have done to her, after all she's been through," said Tamara.

"They are also giving her meds that cause amnesia of the time she has them on board. She won't remember any of the debridement. When she gets off the vent and the 'amnesia medicine,' the psych nurse and Chaplain Rosita Thomas will work with her to resolve her memories of being burned. She'll never forget it, but they can help her not be troubled by the memories of what happened. Why don't we give you a little break and sit in the waiting room for a few minutes?"

"That sounds good, but I hate to leave her," said Tammy.

"Of course, but you need to get out of this heat and humidity for a while. Its draining and this is going to be a long haul." Chaplain Thomas tells family "It's a marathon, not a sprint. You have to pace yourself."

After removing the garb they were wearing over their street clothes (actually, Tom was wearing black scrubs with a large gold cross, his name and Pastoral Care Services embroidered on the breast pocket) and washing off the talcum powder from the gloves, they went to the waiting room.

40

No one else was there and Tom bought them both Diet Cokes from the vending machine.

"That tastes really good," said Tammy after taking a long drink from the can. "It's so hot in there. Why?"

"Our skin is the largest organ of the body. It provides two major functions: To keep in body heat and to keep out infection. When seventy-five percent of that is destroyed, it's a challenge to keep the patient warm and not get infected. They also keep the humidity at about eighty-five percent to reduce dehydration. It's pretty hard on the family and staff, but after a while, you'll get use to it." He paused and then said, "Tell me what happened last night. That must have been pretty awful for everyone."

Tammy nodded, thoughtfully as tears began to roll down her cheeks. Tom sat in silence. She cried a couple of minutes. When she took a deep breath and let out a heavy sigh, he said, "There are a lot of tears to be cried for Diane and this situation. I'm glad you can give yourself permission to let them out. It is important you do as much crying as possible. If you try to bottle up the feelings, it will just come out inappropriately, usually at the worst possible time."

"I do know something about that and I have the D.I.V.O.R.C.E. to prove it," said Tammy as her eyes looked at someplace a long time ago. She was referring to an old Country and Western song, popular in the late Sixties, by Tammy Wynette. "But that was absolutely nothin' compared to the gut kick I got last night. Nothin', and I do mean nothin,' has hurt like this. I just wish I could be the one in that bed, instead of her." New tears began to leak from her swollen eyes. "Am I going crazy, Chaplain? One minute I'm laughing and the next I'm crying. I feel like I'm in a bad dream and I can't wake up."

"You are completely normal. Right now, you're still in shock and many of your emotions are near the surface, so they just 'pop out' with no warning. Does that make sense?"

Tammy nodded, thinking about what the Duty Chaplain had said.

"Tell me what happened last night."

Tammy began to tell her story and Tom led her through an informal

41

debriefing using the same format as he did with the two EMTs.

"I'm going to go back in to be with Diane for awhile. My husband will be here around noon to stay with her and then I'm going home to get some sleep."

"Good plan. It's absolutely essential that you and your husband take good care of yourselves, and each other, so that you can care for Diane and your son. I'll check in on Diane before I go off shift this evening. If I'm not here and you want me to be, for whatever reason, just tell one of the staff. They know how to page me."

01/1043 January 2006

"Trauma team to the trauma room, trauma team to the trauma room," announced the hospital operator as Tom's pager started to vibrate. "I think I just got busy. It has been good talking with you, Tammy. I'm sure I'll see you in another day or so."

"Thank you, for everything," Tammy said and then gave Tom a hug. He walked toward the elevator, trying to not look rushed and wishing he could walk faster. His adrenalin was almost to max level by the time he got to the stairwell, fifty feet from the waiting room. *So much for an easy day.*

CHAPTER 4

03/1507 January 2006

By the time Chaplain (Resident) Sandy Womac, M. Div., walked onto the sixth floor her breathing was slightly labored. She slowed the last hundred steps to the Surgical Intensive Care Unit so that she could "Exude calmness and competence," as Sister Joyce had taught the residents, when going into the code blue to which she was responding. She had bound up two flights from the pediatric unit to which she was assigned. It was her day to carry the duty pager, in addition to her personal one.

As she pushed through the doors, she immediately focused on the bed of a young Hispanic woman surrounded by medicos in various patterns and colors of scrubs. Some wore the white coats of physicians. All had extremely concerned looks as they deftly performed the functions they had done so many times before.

Sandy immediately walked to the head of the patient on the right side, next to the RT, whose face showed relief at the sight of the chaplain. She gave a slight shake of her head saying the patient was not going to make it. Sandy had worked a couple of cases with the Respiratory Therapist and trusted her instincts. She quickly prayed the RT was wrong. One of the nurses was doing CPR as Thaddeus T. Washington, MD ran the code. He quickly glanced at Sandy and confirmed the RT's prognosis. Sandy asked the nurse on the other side of the bed what the name of the patient was.

"Cynthia Gonzalez. Her family is in the waiting room."

Sandy's heart jumped into her throat as she remembered being on call New Year's Eve and visiting with her after she had been transferred from the ER to the Surgical Intensive Care Unit. Now, Cynthia's face was so swollen, and discolored, she didn't recognize her.

"How long has she been down?" asked Thad of no one in particular.

"She coded fifteen minutes ago and we started compressions almost immediately. We've shocked her seven times," replied the nurse next to Sandy.

"I'm open to suggestions," Thad said. "Anyone have any thoughts?" The silence was eerie. "One more time. Three hundred joules," declared Thad. A technician put lubricant jelly on the paddles held by Karl Sassmann, MD, first year resident who came up from the ER with Dr. Washington and Renee Thompson, RN.

"Clear," said Karl much more confidently than he felt. Thoomp! Cynthia's lifeless body convulsed as electricity surged through it. Everyone looked at the heart monitor, expectantly. Flat line. Sandy continued saying the Twenty-third Psalm into Cynthia's ear.

"Again," barked Thad. The procedure was repeated, with the same result. "Call it, Doctor Sassmann."

"Time of death, 1527."

Sandy took a small vile of blessed olive oil, extra virgin, from her pocket, opened it, dabbed a small amount on her thumb and made the sign of the cross on Cynthia's forehead as she said a prayer of blessing and committal for her soul to Almighty God. The staff watched, silently, each deep into their own thoughts. A few crossed themselves as Sandy stepped away from the bed and Thad started thanking everyone for their efforts and expertise. As they began leaving the bedside, the only sound was rubber gloves being pulled off and thrown or dropped into the trash receptacles.

"Chaplain, you ready to go with me?" asked Dr. Sassmann with an almost pleading look.

"Sure," replied Sandy, not looking forward to the next phase of the death protocol.

03/1535 January 2006

Karl Sassmann, MD and Sandy Womack, M. Div. walked into the waiting room and then stood side by side. Both were wearing hospital issue, puke green scrubs. Dr. Sassmann was wearing his physician's white coat and Sandy was wearing a black clergy shirt with Anglican white collar under her scrubs. Cynthia's parents, Alberto and Maria Gonzalez were sitting quietly holding hands. When they looked at the faces of Karl and Sandy, they knew. Maria immediately made the sign of the cross and began to cry and Alberto sat in strained silence. His eyes began to water.

Sandy sat next to Maria as Karl, having had a cultural awareness course for physicians as part of his orientation, addressed Alberto. It was still counter intuitive to his Caucasian sensitivities. "Mr. Gonzalez, quite unexpectedly, Cynthia went into cardiac arrest. Her heart stopped beating and then she quit breathing. We aren't certain, at this point, what caused it, but a code blue was called immediately and we did everything we possibly could to resuscitate her. We were unable to get her back. I'm very sorry."

Alberto collected himself and then said, "Thank you, doctor. We appreciate everything you did. May we see her?"

"Chaplain Womac will take you into the unit in a few minutes, as soon as the staff finishes cleaning up the area."

"Do either of you have any questions for Dr. Sassmann?" Sandy asked, softly. They each thought for a moment and then shook their heads, no.

"I'm sorry for your loss," said Karl. He paused for just a few seconds and then said, "I have something to ask you." We don't know why Cynthia coded, uh, her heart stopped and the only way we, and you, can know for sure is if you give us permission to do a post mortem examination. As her next of kin, we have to have your permission. Would you be willing to sign the release for that?"

"What is that?" asked Alberto.

"It's an autopsy," interjected Sandy. Karl shot her a hostile look as Maria recoiled from the word. She began to weep more openly. Karl continued to stare at Sandy as she said, "It will be helpful to both of you, later, if you know what happened." Karl's look softened only slightly.

The couple began to talk with each other in Spanish. After a few exchanges, Alberto looked at Dr. Sassmann and nodded.

"Thank you," said Karl, "The chaplain will get the paperwork for you to sign. I have to begin rounds in a few moments. If you think of any questions, you can reach me through the hospital."

Now it was Sandy's turn to glare. It was not lost on Karl and he made a mental note to himself to address her intrusion on **his** conversation with *Señor y Señora* Gonzalez. He left with no further comments exchanged.

Sandy sat with the couple for a few more minutes. She felt uncomfortable with the silence, and her thoughts were on what she was going to say to the good doctor the next time she saw him, but, for now, she was determined to do what Sister Joyce had taught, "Sit in silence and simply provide 'ministry of presence.'" For one who thought she was expected to have the answers, even though she knew she did not, it was quite difficult.

"I'm going to go see if they are ready for us to see Cynthia's body." She almost winced as she said it, thinking it too harsh this early in the process, but that was what she had been taught. They nodded their consent and she walked down the hall quickly, relieved to be out of the tension. At least she was *doing* something, now. She moved into the SICU and straight to the bedside where the CNAs were preparing the body. They were almost done. Sandy began to make mental notes of Cynthia's appearance. She waited until the two Certified Nursing Assistants had completed their work.

One of them said, as they were walking away from the bed, "It's just not fair that a beautiful young girl like that should die so unexpectedly.

46

And I heard the Doctor say they broke three of that poor child's ribs doing CPR. It's just not fair, and that's the God's honest truth."

"Ummm huh, you know that's right," replied the other.

Sandy made a mental note to make contact with the women, after the family left, told the charge nurse she was bringing the family in, then went back to the family room. After sitting with Cynthia's parents for a few moments, she softly asked, "Are you ready to see Cynthia?" They both nodded without looking up. "She is not going to look like she did the last time you saw her, so I want to prepare you for what you are about to see."

They nodded, again, still not taking their eyes off the floor. "She will be in the bed she has been in. The covers are pulled up just under her chin. As you may remember, she has one IV in the back of her right hand. During the resuscitation, they had to put a tube in her throat to help her breathe. That can't be removed until they do the autopsy. Also, her coloration has started to change and she will have a slight bluish tint to her skin. If you want to touch her, it's perfectly okay. Do you have any questions?"

The father shook his head "No" and began to stand. He then helped Mrs. Gonzalez to her feet. Sandy went to the woman's other side and gently grasped her arm as they moved toward the door of the family room.

As she walked around the corner from the hallway, she involuntarily caught her breath. She came face to face with Francisco Perez, JD, MBA, CPA for Bolton, Wagner and Kleinschmidt, PA. He was very possibly the most beautiful man she had ever seen. He stood 6'2," had a Copper Tone complexion and piercing brown eyes. His black hair was cut stylishly short and he was dressed in Marx Brothers tan slacks and a cream colored mock turtleneck knit, long sleeve, polo shirt. Maria Gonzalez introduced him as Cynthia's fiancé.

Guilt flooded Sandy as she blushed a deep red. *What kind of jerk am I? He just found out, didn't he, his fiancée is dead and I'm wanting to jump his bones. Get a grip CHAPLAIN!* "I'm sorry to meet you under these circumstances," she stammered.

"What circumstances are those," Francisco asked in a rather testy tone.

Sandy looked at Maria and Alberto. Maria looked away quickly and Alberto just shrugged. Sandy's fear was confirmed. Francisco didn't know that Cynthia was dead. "I think you had better sit down." He looked at her quizzically, but something in her tone indicated he would be wise to follow her direction.

It was hospital procedure that physicians, and only physicians, make death notifications. Sandy reasoned that it would take the good Dr. Sassmann five to ten minutes to answer his page and get back to the waiting area. That was way too long for everyone to sit in silence with Francisco knowing something bad had happened. Sandy was in no mood to play, I-know-something-you-don't-know-and-I-can't-tell-you.

When Francisco sat, she went through the details of what had happened prior to his arrival, watching his nonverbal behavior to see when he was ready for the next piece of information. "They were unable to resuscitate her," Sandy said as her voice trailed off.

"What the hell happened? She was fine when I saw her this morning before I went to the office. When did this happen? How long ago? What happened? This is unreal. I just talked to her a few hours ago."

"This must be quite shocking for you, and totally unexpected. It is for all of us. The doctors don't know what happened except that she went into cardiac arrest. She died about fifteen minutes ago. I was just about to take her parents to see her. Let's give you a few minutes to take this in and then you can go with us, if you wish. I'm going to go see if the staff is ready for us. I'll be right back." Francisco nodded as the information began to register.

Chaplain (Resident) Sandy Womac, M. Div. returned and the four sat in silence for an eternity of about thirty seconds when she heard herself say, "Do you have any questions?"

They each shook their heads in silence. Sandy stood and stepped over to Mrs. Gonzalez to help her stand as her husband did the same on her other side. Francisco sat for a couple of extra seconds, his mind very far away and then stood as if in a stupor. They made their way down the hallway, a portrait of devastating sadness and lack of comprehension. They came to the entrance to the SICU and Sandy paused, looking intently at each of them. "This is going to be very difficult **and** you are going to get through it. Are you ready?" She turned without waiting for a response.

The doors swung open as she hit the metal plate on the wall. The soft hydraulic swoosh mimicked the collective intake of breath as the couple and Francisco walked through it. They instantaneously looked at the curtained area where they had last seen Cynthia. Sandy continued to lead them, then pulled back the curtain just enough for them to enter.

"Aaaayyyyeeeeeeee!" cried the mother as she saw the face of her dead daughter. She continued to sob as she approached the bedside and collapsed over her. The wailing intensified as Maria called her daughter's name. Alberto stood next to her, patting her shoulder, a look of total helplessness on his face. Tears streamed down his cheeks. Sandy continued to stand on Maria's left as she gently slid her hand up her spine several times. The nonverbal prompting helped Maria cry that much harder as she began to make the sounds of a wounded animal. Nonsensical. Primal. "The sound of agony" is what Sr. Joyce called it. It was unnerving for Sandy.

Francisco stood on the other side of the bed, looking down on Cynthia's lifelessness. He began to look at the IV pole with partially used bags, the ventilator, inactive monitors and other medical paraphernalia as if he could somehow make sense of the situation, if he just had enough information. His eyes began to water and one tear ran down his cheek. He turned away from the bed and walked out of the SICU.

Maria's sobs subsided after a few more minutes. Soon, she was crying softly and Alberto awkwardly pulled her head to his chest and wrapped his arms around her. Sandy stood by them, protectively. In time, Maria pulled away, leaned over the bedrails and kissed her daughter on the forehead. Alberto patted Cynthia's hand and kissed her cheek. Then they left the Unit and walked down the corridor holding hands. Sandy directed them into the family room. She waited until they were seated and then announced she was going to find Francisco.

He was not in the waiting room or the corridor. As she began to move back toward the family room, he walked out of the men's room at the far end of the hall. Her next thought had less to do with pastoral care than it did with admiring what a splendid example of a man he was. She was relieved that he hadn't bolted. She walked toward him and asked if he wanted to rejoin Maria and Alberto. He shook his head and asked her to tell them he would be at their home that evening. He turned to leave, hesitated, and then thanked Sandy for her help. He didn't wait for her response. Sandy verbally abused herself for her carnal thoughts all the way back to the family room. *How am I going to tell the IPR group about this one?*, she thought as she wrapped gently on the door and walked into the family room without waiting for a reply.

03/1706 January 2006

"You don't look so good," said Chaplain (Resident) Jaime Martinez, M. Div., as Sandy Womac walked through the door. "Must have been a tough case."

"It was, Jaime. The worst. Do you remember Cynthia Gonzalez? She was the twenty-five year old, Hispanic female you worked with in the trauma room New Year's Eve. I think she was involved in a rollover MVA."

"Yeah, I remember. Her fiancé was there with her parents. Nice family."

"Francisco," Sandy said a bit too quickly—at least to her.

"Who?" asked Jaime.

"Uh, I think the fiancé's name was Francisco." She paused and then said in a less than sincere voice, "I think that was it."

"Yeah, that sounds right. Lawyer type. Quiet and distant. Not in touch with his feelings, as Sister Joyce would say. What the hell happened?"

"They aren't sure. She just went into cardiac arrest and they couldn't

50

get her back. They shocked her nine times after her heart failed, but noth-ing worked."

"You mean she's dead?" asked Jaime, incredulously. "She was pretty banged up, but I don't think anyone anticipated her demise. Thad, Dr. Washington, was pretty positive when they shipped her to SICU. Damn. That just isn't right. She had the world by the tail. It's just not right."

"Yeah, Thad was the doc for the resuscitation. He looked a bit shaken. An enterprising young chaplain resident might make some points if he were just coming on duty and took the time to wander through the ED," said Sandy with a slight smile.

"Well thank you very much, Chuck," said Jaime, his voice dripping with playful sarcasm. "I'm glad you were paying attention when Doctor Charles D. McRae, D. Min., BCC, LPC, Vice President for Pastoral Care Services, MMHS presented his class. I am truly impressed at your ability for retention of the spoken word." Now they were both smiling broadly and the sadness in the room had dissipated, somewhat.

"Think I'm going to go home and get drunk," said Sandy.

"Yeah, I heard Sister say she's been meaning to talk to you about that drinking problem you have. What are you up to these days? One and a half glasses of chardonnay before you pass out?"

"Oh, it's much worse than that. Sometimes I finish the second glass before I toddle off to bed."

"That's what I'm talking about. Alcoholism is a progressive dis-ease. It takes more and more to kill all those brain cells." They were both chuckling, now.

"I'm out of here. *Hasta luego.* Hope you have a good night," said Sandy with new sincerity in her voice.

"Don't stand in the door or you'll get run over. I'm leaving, too."

"I thought you had the duty, tonight."

"Nope. I have the SAFE call. I'm heading home once I've read the log."

"Well I really hope you don't get called. Those cases are always tough. I dread it when I'm on the roster. There's just too much evil in this world," said Sandy, reflectively. "See you when I see you." She walked out the door, thinking about Francisco Perez, MBA. *Damn, girl. You gotta knock this shit off. It is getting you nowhere.* Then, she began to think of Karl Sassman, MD. *Arrogant pig.*

"Hey chaplain, got a minute?" Sandy shuddered as she recognized the voice of one of the nurses from the ED.

I just want to go home, Sandy thought to herself. "Sure. What's up?"

04/0323 January 2006

Chaplain (Resident) Jaime Martinez, M. Div. punched in the "secret code," i.e., not known by patients and their family members, to the ER sliding doors on the key pad of Methodist Specialty Hospital while trying to wipe the sleep from his eyes. Thirty minutes earlier he was slumbering soundly next to Maria when the SAFE pager went off. "SAFE CASE JUST AR-RIVED."

"She's still with the police officer. It's an SAPD case. They should be through shortly. Want some coffee, Chaplain?" asked the nurse behind the counter of the ER nurses' station.

"That would be wonderful. Thank you," said Jaime. Just then, Je-niece Taylor, RN walked up to Jaime. She was the specially trained SAFE nurse who would be doing the forensic evidence exam on San Antonio's latest reported rape victim.

Methodist Specialty Hospital had the contract with SAPD, Bexar County Sheriff's Department and several surrounding counties' law en-forcement agencies to provide forensic exams for the collection of legal evidence. Since the program began eighteen months earlier, the convic-tion rate for sexual assault in Bexar County had increased by two point three percent. It was considered a major success by law enforcement and the county attorney's office.

When Kathy Watts, RN, the ER nurse manager, first presented the idea to the hospital administrators, she defined the response team as a SAFE nurse, volunteer patient advocate from the San Antonio Rape Crisis Services Center and a chaplain from the MMHS staff. Everyone agreed.

Trevor G. Conyers, D. Min., BCC, LPC, LMFT, Director of Clinical Chaplaincy Services and the rest of the PCS team hand-selected those who would receive the additional training and serve on the duty roster. Sandy Womac and Jaime Martinez were the first two Residents to ever be accepted for the program. Heretofore, only Clinicians, Directors and Charles had served in that capacity.

"The RCSC volunteer will be a little late because she lives about thirty minutes out. The police are just finishing taking the report, so you and I can start with the survivor in just a minute," said Jeniece to Jaime. Just then they heard the door open to the outer room of the SAFE suite. They turned, simultaneously toward it as a familiar female police officer walked into the hallway and stopped. As soon as the nurse and chaplain reached the door, she nodded, stepped away and started walking toward the nurses' station. Jeniece and Jaime walked in and he closed the door.

An eighteen year old Caucasian girl/woman was sitting on one of the two small couches with a blanket wrapped around her shoulders. Her blouse was torn slightly and her face had an abrasion on her right cheek and the beginning of a bruise on her left forehead. Jeniece introduced herself and sat next to the victim who was eyeing Jaime suspiciously.

Next to her on the other end of the couch sat a twenty year old Caucasian male who identified himself as the survivor's boy friend. "Heather and I are students at UTSA (University of Texas at San Antonio). Her parents are on their way. They live in Pleasanton and will be here in about an hour." His face was a study in concern, stress and helplessness.

"Hello, I'm Chaplain Jaime Martinez and I'm a part of the Sexual Assault Forensic Evidence team. The patient advocate will be here shortly." Looking at Heather, Jaime said, "I'm very sorry for what has happened to you this evening. The nurse will do the first part of the information collection and then I will continue by doing an informal debriefing with you while she prepares the examination room." The young woman continued

53

to stare at him as though she was trying to decide if he was someone she could trust.

Jeniece began by asking the patient's name, age, address and other relevant data. The she said, "Tell us what happened this evening." Pause. "Take your time and use whatever language you are most comfortable with."

"She just told the police officer what happened. You can get the information from her," said the young man.

"I know this must seem confusing for you, but I need to hear it from her in case I have to testify in court, later," said Jeniece. Jaime started to add something, but decided to wait. Heather reluctantly began telling her story. She had been at a school social event with several friends and then decided to go get something more substantial to eat than the snacks at the party.

One of the three college boys at the event offered to take her home after dinner and she agreed. By the time she got to the car she was feeling light headed and "felt my body was getting heavier with each step. I passed out as soon as I got in the car. The next thing I knew, I woke up in what turned out to be his bed in the apartment he shared with two other college guys. I was naked and sore, 'down there,'" Heather said. "I just had a sheet covering me." She began to cry, softly.

Jaime looked at the boyfriend, who had by now introduced himself as Cameron Torrington and clarified that he was not with Heather at the party. "I was studying because I'm taking a winter session course, right now. Heather stayed in San Antonio during the break because she is working at the GAP in La Ventana Mall. She also doesn't really like Pleasanton," added Cameron. His eyes had begun to water and he had blushed a bright red when Heather talked about waking in a strange bed.

Jeniece waited for him to finish. "We will draw some blood to test for whether or not you were given one of the date rape drugs." She then went on to explain what would happen in the exam and why they were doing it. She continued writing on the report form and asked some specific questions about penetration, where it had occurred and if any "foreign objects" had been used. Most of Heather's answers were vague and she had great difficulty remembering much of what happened.

"Thank you for saying what happened. I know it's hard to do that, and you did it well," said Jeniece.

"I'm sorry I couldn't remember more," said Heather.

"It's okay. Over the next few days you may have more memories. When you do, be sure you write them down in a journal or notebook so you can tell the police. I'm going to prepare the exam room now, and the chaplain will talk with you while I do. The most important thing for you to remember is that none of this is your fault."

"I never should have gone in that car with him. I only met him that night. That was really stupid," Heather said with contempt in her voice. She began to cry, again. Cameron dropped her hand that he was holding and put his arm around her as she began to sob. Jaime maintained eye contact with him and nodded approval of how he was being supportive of Heather.

When she had stopped crying, a few minutes later, Jaime said, "If you're ready, I would like to walk you through an informal debriefing. Research indicates that this is helpful to people who have been traumatized. You have already completed the first part which is to share what happened.

There was a light rap on the door as it opened and Charla Ratzliff burst into the room. She was quite flustered and immediately dominated the setting. "I'm so sorry to be late. I hope you haven't started without me. I got here as fast as I could, but there is a lot of fog and I had to drive very slowly." Catching her breath, she introduced herself to the young couple who were emotionally frozen by the interruption. Charla sat down on the edge of the couch with half her morbidly obese bottom hanging off of it. She took a deep breath and asked, "What happened, tonight?"

Jaime immediately replied, "Jeniece has done her initial interview and I was just beginning to do the rest of the debriefing. She's getting the room ready for the exam." Charla opened her mouth to say something as Jaime continued, "I think it would be best if you catch your breath while we do the forensic exam and then you can share your information after that. Her parents should be arriving any time and you can stay with them and Cameron while I do." His tone of voice, while caring, left little doubt that he was responsible for the next steps in the protocol.

Jaime had worked a couple of other cases with Charla. She was not his favorite volunteer. In his opinion, she seemed to make everything about her. He had actually complained to her supervisor once, after clearing it with Sister Joyce. He had seen no positive results or changes from his having done so. He was impressed and felt comfortable with all the other volunteers from RCSC. He never quite understood why Charla was allowed to remain one.

"I know you don't remember much and that's normal. Please share with me what thoughts you had during those times you can remember." Jaime continued to walk her through the other four steps and then shared with her and Cameron the ever present brochure listing the cognitive, behavioral, physical, emotional and spiritual signs of response to trauma that Charles McRae had redacted early in his career as a Licensed Professional Counselor. It had become a useful tool to educate chaplains, therapists, survivors and family members.

Jeniece came out of the exam room just as Jaime was finishing his explanation of the brochure. She sat in one of the other two chairs in the well-appointed "parlor" outside the exam room. One of the wealthy matrons of MMHS had paid for the furniture and accouterments. "We want to have as comfortable and inviting a space as possible for the survivors and their families," Charles said when he made the "ask." He knew this was an issue she had championed before and suspected she or a family member had been through a similar experience.

"We're ready to do the exam," Jeniece said to Heather. "Chaplain will join us and I will tell him when to face the wall with his back to you. I will talk you through everything I do and why. Let's go on in." Jaime knew she had also worked with Charla and had had an equally negative experience. She once reported that the volunteer had actually corrected her procedure during the exam. *Not a way to win friends or influence enemies,* thought Jaime, at the time.

The exam room was the usual sterile environment found in hospitals throughout the country. There were no amenities. There was a particularly large, sophisticated camera sitting on the sink counter along with the usual glass containers of long swabs, cotton balls, alcohol dispensers, etc. The gynecological exam table dominated the room. Two "physician" stools on casters were the only other furniture. On the walls were a couple of pictures of pastoral scenes and a medical chart of the female reproductive system.

"Chaplain, you can face the wall, now," said Jeniece. "Heather, I need you to stand on this white butcher paper and take off all your clothing. We will give you something to wear home after we're through in here. We have to keep your clothes as evidence and for DNA testing. We do this with all the survivors."

The term survivor was used by all members of the SAFE team after the debriefing to reaffirm the person's power and to negate the self image of a victim. Just like in television shows, it was repeatedly emphasized that what happened was not their fault. As Chaplain Trevor Conyers, D. Min., BCC, LMFT, LPC, Director of Clinical Chaplaincy Services said, on numerous occasions, out of the earshot of survivors and family members, "Rape is not a suitable punishment for being stupid."

Jaime then heard her getting on the exam table and putting her feet in the stirrups. "I have a nice warm blanket to cover you with," said Jeniece. "You can turn around now, Chaplain." Jaime pulled up one of the two stools and sat on it, facing Heather with his back to Jeniece. Heather's legs were draped with a warm sheet. "I'm going to examine you from head to toe to see if there are any contusions, cuts, scrapes or bruises. I will manipulate the blanket so that your privacy will not be violated. If I do find any, I will document it on this chart." She held a clip board with a sheet of paper with anterior and posterior drawings of the female body. I will also need to take pictures."

Heather's eyes widened and Jaime placed his hand on her wrist, after he had asked her permission to do so. "The pictures cannot be used in any way to identify you. They will only be of the injuries. When she photographs the scrapes on your face, it will be specific and limited. You cannot be identified."

Heather began to breathe, again, and her expression was calmer. "Why did I have to tell Jeniece what happened after I had just told the police officer?" asked Heather.

"Because, if she is called to testify in court at the perpetrators' trial, she has to be able to say you told her what happened. Otherwise, it is hearsay and therefore, inadmissible. No one designed it this way, but it's also important to tell your story as many times as possible to facilitate the healing process. It's called catharsis. Are you familiar with that term?" She shook her head. "It is from the Greek and means to cleanse or to clean. When we express our feelings by talking about them and the painful experiences that caused them, we are literally cleansing our bodies of the toxins the feelings create.

"Does that make sense?" he asked. She nodded. Jaime continued talking with her during the remainder of the exam. He was using the old dentist trick of keeping her distracted. He asked if she had remembered anything else about the assault. She looked at the ceiling as she thought about the question. "I remember hearing two male voices discussing what they were planning to do to me. It was totally obscene. I felt sick to my stomach and then I passed out, again. The next thing I remember is one of them was on top of me but I couldn't move. I wanted to scream, but I couldn't. I just started shaking my head back and forth trying to get him to stop." Pause. "I can remember feeling him inside me. It hurt. I am a virgin." Pause. "Or, I was." She began to cry, softly, as Jaime asked if he could place his hand on her shoulder. She nodded and he did so. He knew she had begun the healing process as she allowed herself to remember the traumatizing experience. He reassured her by gently squeezing her shoulder.

Jeniece was quite good to walk her through the process. "Okay, I'm going to insert the speculum, now. You may feel a slight pinch. I warmed it so it would be a little more comfortable for you." Pause. "I have the swabs I need and I'm going to remove it now. That's all we need to do. You can take your feet out of the stirrups and rest your legs on the table," she said as she pulled the extension out of the table on which Heather was laying. "Thank you, Chaplain, you can step out now, so Heather can get dressed." Jeniece began taking a set of scrubs, bra and panties out of a small cabinet as she asked Heather what sizes she wore. "These clothes are a gift of the Rape Crisis Services Center here in San Antonio." Jaime closed the door behind him as he walked into the "Parlor." A middle aged couple sat on the couch with Cameron. Charla sat in one of the arm chairs.

"Mr. and Mrs. McClaren?" asked Jaime. They nodded as if they were in a heavy, sound inhibiting, fog. "I'm Chaplain Jaime Martinez. The SAFE nurse, Jeniece, just finished the forensic examination. Heather did very well and she wanted me to tell you that she did not have any significant **physical** injuries. She will be out in a few moments."

"You were with her?" asked the father, somewhat indignantly.

"Yes. Our research has shown that the sooner a survivor can begin to bond with other men, the better their recovery is and the fewer negative projections there are to **all** men. The survivor's modesty and privacy are never violated when the chaplain is male," explained Jaime. Mr. McClaren continued to be a bit skeptical, but said nothing more.

"When will we be able to see her?" asked Ms. McClaren.

"In just a few more minutes. She's getting dressed now," said Jaime. *Clearly, she's still in the shock phase of her grief. Guess we better help her get to the "expression of emotions" stage*, he thought to himself. "Please share with me how you found out Heather was here."

Mr. McClaren cleared his throat and said hoarsely, "The San Antonio police called and said she had been, uh, assaulted and was at Methodist Specialty Hospital. Once we got to the city it seemed to take forever to find it. The nurse at the desk in the Emergency Room walked us to here. She was nice. Charla, here, has been telling us what happened and what the Rape Center can do to help Heather."

Great, Charla, let's have a HIPAA violation of sharing private information of an adult with her parents, thought Jaime. "I know this has been a horrible shock for you and is very painful. I'm sorry." He then took them through a quick debriefing on hearing the news and shared *The* pamphlet with them. They were reading the back page which had a list of suggestions on how to help someone who has recently been traumatized when the door to the examination room opened. As Heather walked into the "parlor" her parents stood, embraced her and all three began to cry. No words were necessary. Jaime stood behind the parents with a hand on a shoulder of each.

"Why don't you have a seat and I will give you a few discharge instructions and you can leave," said Jeniece when the crying had subsided. She began to hand medication bottles to Heather with verbal instructions in addition to the ones written thereon. She also had her take some of the meds immediately explaining they were to prevent pregnancy and any Sexually Transmitted Infections she may have contracted from the rapist or rapists. Mom doubled over as though struck in the abdomen and began to cry, again. Jeniece paused until she sat up. Dad had lovingly put his arm around her as his eyes moistened.

"The last thing I need to tell you is that in about a month, you need to be tested for HIV and then again in six months," said Jeniece. Heather had a shocked look as she began to process the information just given. New tears began to roll down her cheeks as she realized the implications of the guidance. Mom and Dad just went into shock, again.

The parents, survivor and boyfriend all stood and began to gather their coats and other belongings. Jaime walked them to the emergency room exit while giving them his card and telling them, in a very pastoral tone, to call him if he could be useful to them in the future. Saying goodbye produced more feelings of helplessness and pain than usual for him. He turned and went back through the ER to the SAFE suite. *I gotta talk to Charla's supervisor. This crap has got to stop or they need to fire her,* thought Jaime.

A second nurse was telling Jeniece that two suspects and a SAPD officer were tucked away in a room waiting for her to do a forensic exam on the two college age students. "Great, I just love pulling pubic hairs on those SOBs," said Jeniece while rolling her eyes. Jaime had always thought doing an exam on suspects should be done by a second SAFE nurse because it seemed like cruel and unusual punishment--for the nurse who had just examined the survivor.

CHAPTER 5

04/1420 January 2006

"Fuck."

That was all the twenty-something, petite, Resident II said, to no one other than herself, as she walked out of the hospital room on the pediatric unit. She, along with a team from the Emergency Department and her staff, had been unsuccessful in resuscitating a seven year old Caucasian boy who had gone into spontaneous respiratory arrest. He was recovering from pneumonia and had been within normal limits in his progression. So much so, that neither of his parents was present when the arrest occurred.

Simple eloquence, thought Chaplain John Allison, D. Min., BCC. The doctor left him as the only living occupant in the room. He knew one of the CNAs and probably an LVN would return as soon as they had collected themselves. A "pedi" death was always hard on the staff. One so unexpected was even harder. After a short prayer over the child's lifeless body, John left to begin "catching butterflies" at the nurses' station. That's what Charles D. McRae, D. Min., BCC, LPC had called it during an in-service with the chaplain residents. It was his Pastoral Care 101 class that he taught each year to the new class of CPE students. John was the next presenter and had arrived a few minutes early.

As he walked down the corridor he began preparing himself for the death notification to the parents and the subsequent process. *There's just got to be an easier way to make a living,* he thought to himself.

As John sat in the nurses' station, sipping a cup of coffee, one of the Licensed Vocational Nurses drifted toward him and said, "That was a really tough one, wasn't it Chaplain?"

"Yes it **is**."

"It don't seem I'll ever get used to it. I just hate it when we lose one that way. It's just not right.

"It seems very unfair."

"He was such a pretty child, with his whole life in front of him. His parents will be just devastated. I don't know how one ever gets over something like that. I don't think I could. One time my Trei, he's George C. Greenman III, was hospitalized for pneumonia. He was only two years old and was already on antibiotics for **another** ear infection. I hadn't been to nurses training and I was scared to death. I just kept praying, "Sweet Jesus, protect my boy." The three days he was there were the longest I have ever had. I just can't imagine what it must be like to lose one. Days like today, I wish I worked on the geriatric ward. Those people have lived long lives and are just waitin' to die. Why does God have to go and take one of these children? Just don't seem right. No sir, it just don't seem right."

"It feels like the earth just moved, or something," added John.

"You know that's right. My Trei is fourteen now, but when I get home, I'm going to give him an extra hug and fix his favorite dinner." She paused, weighing whether or not to continue. "Sometimes when something like this happens, I go into his room when he's asleep and I pray over him and ask the Good Lord to please don't let no harm come to him. It would just break my heart if it did." She studied the chaplain to see if he would be critical of her confession.

"When my children were young, I would do the same thing. I would make the sign of the cross over them when they were sleeping and then thank God for them. It's always scary to think of something happening to our own, like we see here."

"That is the God's honest truth. But I guess I'll get through this one, too. I always seem to, somehow." Pause. "Listen to me, 'somehow.' God's always there to pick us up when we're down. Isn't he, Chaplain?"

"Yes, God is always there. That's a great promise, isn't it?"

"It sure enough is. Thank you for talking with me, Chaplain. You always say the right thing. Guess I better get back to work. See you around, Chaplain; and thanks again."

The nurse quietly moved down the hall, softly singing a religious hymn to herself. John just shook his head and made a big sigh as he contemplated the power of listening. *If all of the job was this easy, everyone would want to do it.* He silently chuckled to himself as he headed toward the office of the Director of Clinical Chaplaincy Services to log the death. He hoped there wouldn't be anyone there. He was just too drained to engage in banal chit chat.

Chaplain John Allison's pager went off a second later. "Code Blue, CCU, room five. Code Blue, CCU, room five," came over the public address system. Taking a deep breath, he began to move toward the stair well to drop three flights to the Cardiac Care Unit. *Sorry knees, the elevators are just too damned slow this time of day*, he thought to himself as he entered the stair well. This was one of the ICUs for which he was responsible. He also had the Medical ICU.

04/1542 January 2006

John walked past several gawkers staring through the glass wall from the hallway and into room five in the Cardiac Care Unit to a familiar site. Three docs, two Registered Nurses, one Respiratory Therapist, and a Nurse's Aide were busily performing the necessary functions for a "full code." He recognized the Nurse Manager as she brushed passed him with two viles of blood to be sent to the lab, "stat."

At least some things remain constant, he thought. He noticed a seventy-something Hispanic woman sitting in a wheel chair quietly crying as two women in their late forties or early fifties attended her. *No doubt the wife and probably daughters. This ain't going to be easy.*

"Padre, he's sick nigh unto Jesus. You better start hanging the crepe with the family," said Thaddeus T. Washington, MD. John nodded as he approached the patient on the other side of the bed from Thad. He slipped between the RT preparing a respirator for use and the RN doing chest compressions. He quietly said to them, "If I get in your way, I'll trade places with you." They nodded their assent.

"Do we know what his faith tradition is?" asked John.

"He's Catholic and he has been anointed by a priest" said the RN who had been taking care of him the last two days." I documented the chart this morning when Father Carlos made rounds."

"Thanks, Nancy. I really appreciate your being on top of that. It makes life a whole lot easier."

"Just doing what you taught me, Chaplain."

John smiled slightly as he remembered the resistance he got when he had done a ten minute in-service with the nurses during shift change on the importance of documenting religious rights administered to patients. Nancy was one of the last to accept yet another responsibility to the already too long list of tasks. The turning point was when she overheard a new widow tell John how much it meant to her to know that her recently departed husband had been anointed and received the Eucharist the morning of his death.

The Chaplain leaned over, introduced himself to the patient and said into his ear, "The Lord is my shepherd, I shall not want...." As trained, he said it loud enough for the entire staff to hear. When he finished saying the Psalm, two nurses and a Doctor crossed themselves and all the others bowed their heads ever so briefly.

Dr. Washington said quietly, "Stop compressions." Everyone looked at the monitor. It was a flat line. "How long have we been doing CPR?" the doctor asked.

"Eighteen minutes" said the RN functioning as recorder.

"How many times have we shocked him?"

"Six."

"Dr. Sassmann, please call it," said Thad, almost reverently.

"Time of death, 1604," said Karl Sassmann, MD in the same tone.

"Dr. Sassmann, the good chaplain will go with you to inform the family. Try to get a post," Thad said as he began to exit the glass cubicle.

It always amazed John how quickly a room emptied after a code was called. The staff just seemed to melt away. He looked at the young Dr. Sassmann and nodded his head toward the door as he gestured with his left hand for Karl to precede him.

Once in the corridor, the Nurse Manager walked up and announced that she had put the family in the nurse's lounge and began to lead the solemn pair towards it, knowing full well John had been there many times.

As soon as the three women saw the doctor, Nurse Manager and chaplain walk through the door, they burst into tears. Katy Ballenger, RN reached for a box of tissues to give the family as the doctor sat on the lone remaining chair so he could look directly into the eyes of the wife, now widow, still sitting in the hospital wheel chair that Katy insisted she use rather than stand in the hallway.

The women were still crying as the Intern started to speak. Chaplain John Allison, D. Min., BCC gently touched his arm and silently shook his head, slightly. The family didn't see the exchange. Sassmann swallowed hard and was anything but a picture of serenity, but he didn't say anything. Now he was watching John for his cue as to when he could speak. Just then the wife reached for a tissue, blew her nose and dabbed at her tears. Just as subtly, John nodded and Dr. Sassmann cleared his throat and began to speak.

"Mrs. Garibay, as you know, your husband went into cardiac arrest a little earlier and we began resuscitation procedures almost immediately. We did everything we could to save your husband, but we were unsuccessful." The woman looked at the young physician as though she did not understand what he was saying and then began to sob deeply. The two daughters followed her lead and the three embraced and cried and touched and cried and wiped away each other's tears.

"He was getting better," said Mrs. Garibay in an accusatory tone. "The other doctor said, this morning, that he was getting better. What happened? What happened? *Madre de Dios. ¿Por qué, por qué?*

Once again the doctor began to speak and once again, the chaplain gently touched his arm indicating for him to wait. The woman and her daughters cried some more. Then she looked up and the chaplain nodded at Karl.

"Mrs. Garibay, we don't know what happened. Apparently, he was getting better, but when they called us in the ER, his heart had stopped. We did everything we could. I'm sorry we were not successful in resuscitating your husband." This time, he quit talking without prompting when she lowered her head and cried. When Mrs. Garibay looked up, he continued, "In order for you and us to know what happened to cause his expiration, we need your consent to perform a post mortem examination."

"You mean an autopsy?" the older of the daughters asked.

"Yes, an autopsy. The nurse will get the paper work for you to give your consent. It's the only way ya'll will know what happened, and it may well help us to understand how to better care for patients, in the future. It will help others like your husband."

The older woman looked at each of her daughters as if to say, "Tell me what to do."

"Mumi, I think Daddy would have said yes," offered the younger daughter. The elder nodded affirmatively, but said nothing. The mom thought for a moment and nodded also.

Karl started to get up and John quickly said, "Do you have any questions of the doctor before he returns to his other duties?" The three women shook their heads as they continued to cry softly.

"If you think of something later, you can call me here at the hospital. Just ask for Doctor Sassmann. I'm very sorry for your loss," he added, awkwardly. Then he stood and walked out the door.

"I'll go get the papers for you to sign," Katy announced as she headed for the door. "Can I get you anything, some water or coffee?" Again, the three just shook their heads.

67

"What did you hear the doctor say?" John asked.

Mrs. Garibay said, unkindly, "He said my Roberto is dead." And then she started to cry, again. John sat in silence as the daughters tried to comfort their mother. Then the older one spoke, "He also said that we need to let them do an autopsy. That's the only way they, I mean we, will know what happened to him. At first I didn't like the idea, but if it helps someone else, then I guess it's okay."

Katy lightly rapped the door as she walked in. She sat in the chair the Intern had vacated and extended a clip board with some forms on it to the older woman. She used her pen to point to each paragraph as she explained what Mrs. Garibay's options were. "You can limit the autopsy in any way you wish," she said. "If you don't want them to examine the head, you can say that."

"If they do it, can we still have the casket open?" inquired the younger daughter.

"Absolutely," replied Katy. There will be no visual disfigurement."

"Mumi, do you want him buried in his blue suit or his brown cowboy shirt and slacks with the western buckle?" asked daughter number one.

The woman seemed to age before John's eyes as she began to grasp the reality of what she was about to go through. "*No se. Tarde, más tarde.*"

"Yes, that's right. You don't have to make that decision right now. You can discuss it after you get home and have had some time to absorb all this," said John. "Right now, we only need to sign the papers and then if you want, I can take you in to see Roberto's body before you leave." John never felt completely comfortable using the term "body" so early in the process, but he knew from many similar experiences that what appeared to be a minor unkindness would, over time, help the family get through their grief process faster and in a more healthy fashion.

"Yes, I want to see him before I go," Mrs. Garibay said as new tears streamed down her face.

"You only have to sign this one document for the 'post,' I mean autopsy and then we have one other to sign, if you know which funeral home you want to use. If not, you can call us later and just tell us to whom we are to release the body," said Katy.

"Mumi, you want to use Martinez and Martinez, don't you?" asked daughter number one.

"Yes. They were there for us with *Abuelita y Abuelito*. *Señor* Martinez and his son are kind. I like them."

"Just sign here, and here," Katy directed. She took back the clip board and silently handed it to John to sign as witness. "Is there anything I can do for you, before I leave?"

Just then, the quiet hum of John's pager was heard by all. He pulled it from his belt and read the scrolling text: "Family of peds pt eta 15 minutes." *This is going to be tight. Should I call in reinforcements? No, I can do this.* John began to prepare the Garibays for the viewing of their husband/father. "Are you ready? We can come back here to catch your breath, if you wish." *Please say no.*

"I think it best if we just leave from his room. We'll be alright," offered daughter number two.

"As you wish," said John. *Thank you Jeeeeeezus!* "I will be right back. I want to be sure everything is ready." He left the room and walked as fast as he thought seemly to view the body and make sure everything was in order. He was relieved to find that it was.

When Chaplain Allison returned to the nurses' lounge, the older daughter nodded they were ready and he walked the women down the corridor. As they went around the curtain into the ICU cubicle, Mrs. Garibay gave a quiet gasp upon seeing her husband of fifty-two years lifeless body on the bed. The sheets were neatly pulled to just under his chin, his eyes were closed and his mouth was only slightly open. *Much better than many I've seen*, thought John.

"I want you to know that one of our priests, Father Carlos, anointed Roberto this morning. And, I said the Shepherd's Psalm to him during the resuscitation." John waited until Mrs. Garibay's eyes told him she was ready to hear more. "I was with him, holding his hand when the doctor pronounced him. Then, Doctor Sassmann, Katy, and I came to tell you he was gone."

69

"Thank you," said the older daughter.

"Would you like to have a prayer before we leave?" asked John.

"Yes, please," said the same daughter. They all three crossed themselves as they bowed their heads and closed their eyes. John finished the prayer in the name of the triune God. Once again the Garibay's crossed themselves.

After a moment of silence, Mrs. Garibay turned to leave and the daughters each kissed the forehead of their father's body and followed their mother. John walked them to the elevator as his pager buzzed, again. The other family was here.

"I pray things will go as well for you as they possibly can. If I may be of any further service, please call me," he said as he handed the older daughter his business card. She immediately gave him a tight frontal hug as she ran her hands over his behind. She then stepped into the elevator with her family as though nothing had happened. *Well that sure as hell doesn't happen every day. In fact it's never happened, to me, at least. I feel slimed.*

As soon as the doors closed, he turned and sprinted to the stair well and then up the three flights two steps at a time.

04/1652 January 2006

John walked onto the pediatric unit just as the nurses were taking the family into the unit consultation room. He fell into line just as one of the nurses began to close the door. The pediatric hospitalist on duty began to explain that their son had gone into respiratory arrest, a code was called and the resuscitation was unsuccessful. "I'm very sorry," said the doctor as he wiped a tear from his eye. The petite Resident II simply reached over and put her hand on the shoulder of the mom. Tears streamed down the faces of both women.

The mom leaned into her husband and began to sob. The father just sat, his arm around his wife's shoulders, in a total state of shock. His

70

face had blanched and he was as white as the proverbial sheet.

John moved from where he was leaning against the wall next to the door and walked to the far side of the couple, next to the dad. After a moment, he gently laid his hand on the man's shoulder. Dad's head bowed and his body convulsed in sobs. The couple held each other, tightly, for a seemingly long time. The staff sat in silence as they looked at everything in the room except the couple. John removed his hand from the man's shoulder when his crying began to soften. Eventually, they both looked up and began to wipe their tears. "May we see him?" asked the father.

All of the staff looked at the chaplain. "We'll go to his room as soon as the doctor finishes talking with you. He has a couple of questions to ask, and I'm sure you have some for him."

"We did everything we could and we don't know what happened to cause him to quit breathing. We would like to perform an autopsy," said the doctor.

"Whatever needs to be done to find out what happened," said the mom. She paused, collected her thoughts and then said, "We thought we would be taking him home, tomorrow. I just can't believe this is happening."

"It must seem like a bad dream," reflected John.

"Yes. I keep thinking I'll wake up…but I know I won't."

"It's just too much to grasp, right now," said John. Pause. "Do you have any questions for the doctor?"

"No. Can we see him now?"

"I'm very sorry for your loss. Please call me if I can do anything else," said the doctor. Then he excused himself and left the room, quietly. The Resident followed. One of the nurses left after offering her condolences. John excused himself and said he would be right back.

He went into the boy's room to insure the body was ready and refresh his memory on how he looked. Then he went back to the consultation room, prepared the parents to see their son's body with the breathing tube still in his mouth and the IV lines in place. He had started to turn blue and John reported that as well. They all sat in silence until the mom

71

stood and announced she was ready. The father followed, still in the stupor of grief.

Each gasped as the door to their son's room swung open and they saw his lifeless body. The wife stopped in the middle of the room, unable to move closer. With her husband on one side and the chaplain on the other she stood perfectly still trying to absorb the horror before her. Tears streamed down her face as her lower lip quivered. She shook her head, slightly, and then walked to her son's dead body. John was with her step for step. The father followed, fighting the urge to bolt from the room and run screaming down the corridor.

Mom gently reached out to touch her son's cheek with the back of her fingers. Then she leaned over and kissed him and turned to walk out.

"Is there anything you would like to say to him?" asked John. The woman looked at the chaplain as though she was completely unaware that he was capable of speech. She turned back to the bed and said, "I love you. I'm so sorry I wasn't here with you." She began to sob as she fell into her husband's arms. He held her with absolutely no cognitive awareness of where he was or what he was doing. His numbness was complete.

Again, John gently placed his hand on the man's shoulder as he said softly, "it's okay to cry. I know this hurts really bad." The dam broke and the two held each other even more tightly as they sobbed out their pain. John led them to the two chairs in the room when there was a lull in their crying. They sat for a long time in complete silence.

"What do we need to do now?" asked the father. He said it softly, but his wife reacted as though a cannon had just been discharged. John explained they needed to sign the consent form for the autopsy and the release of the body to a funeral home. He quickly added that if they didn't know which mortuary they wanted to use, they could just sign the document and call in their decision once it had been made.

"If you're ready, I'll go get the papers." The father nodded, silently. John went to the nurses' station and informed the attending RN the family was ready to do the paper work. He returned to the parents quietly talking in the room with their dead son's body a few feet away. Both of them acknowledged John's presence *sans* words. Two minutes later, the nurse walked in with the necessary papers on a clip board. Once signed, the couple stood to leave, each one pausing momentarily at their son's bedside. After a few more tears, they walked out of the room. John accompanied them to the elevator. His words felt hollow as he realized they weren't hearing anything he was saying. *Guess it's a wash. That REALLY sucked. Glad it's over. For them, it's just beginning.* John breathed a short prayer for the couple as he headed to the chaplain's office to log in his day's activities, having walked them to the front door of the hospital. *Guess I don't have to feel guilty about cashing my paycheck, today.*

04/1803 January 2006

"If you were more efficient, you'd get your work done by five o'clock, like everyone else," Charles D. McRae, D. Min., BCC, LPC said with a big grin as John walked into the office of Clinical Chaplaincy.

"Back atcha," John said, his mood beginning to lighten. "I didn't think people of your station in life ever worked this late." He was smiling.

"Just thought I'd check the log before I went home. The Leaders' Council ran long—as per usual. Some people just never seem to tire of pole vaulting over mushrooms. The money the System spends for meetings like that."

"Anything significant happen?" John now had a large grin on his face.

"Nope. Just samo-samo. Do more with less and keep a close tab on how many paper clips we're using. I guess that's not really fair. We did talk about opening the new hospital in New Braunfels."

"How many new FTEs will we get?" asked John.

"Bill (William F. Groene, FACHE and CEO of MMHS) and I agreed on three clinical chaplains, out of house PRN (as needed) duty chaplains and a part time admin support person, probably twenty hours per week. I hope to grow that into 3.5 FTEs of chaplain and one full time support staff. The problem with that is finding half a priest." John smiled. "Depends on how fast they can fill the beds and how much revenue the new site will produce. We have the potential for an AADC (Adjusted average daily census, a prorated combination of inpatients and outpatients per day) of 350 with a level two ED and 250 inpatient beds. Of course, the bean counters will want to whittle that down, but I think we can get what we're asking for—if the numbers support it."

"I'm impressed," said John. "Any idea who you'll be putting out there, or will you put new hires there?"

"Not a clue. I have to talk with Trevor (Trevor G. Conyers (LTC-RET USA), D. Min., BCC, LMFT, Director of Clinical Chaplaincy Services, MMHS) and then advertise the positions and see what we come up with. If we get an experienced keeper we might put them out there, or it may make better sense to send a couple of MMHS veterans there since they know how the System works and Trevor's quirks—not to suggest in any way he's not almost as competent as his boss."

"Certainly not, *Jefe*." John was smiling broadly, now. The tension had drained from his face and he was his usual, calm self.

"If we get a couple of less experienced chaplains, we'll put them at the Mother Ship." Charles was referring to Mercy Methodist Hospital, the flagship of the System. "I'll get out of your hair, if you had any, and let you finish what you came here to do and go home. Can I buy you dinner? Beth is at a conference and I'm batching."

"Thanks, but I promised dad I'd drop by the nursing home after work. I'll take a rain check."

"*No problema, amigo.* See you tomorrow," Charles said as he got up to leave. *That's called care for the care giver. I'm glad it seemed to help. Wish I had a dozen of him. We could do some serious good. I wonder if John would like to be the lead chaplain at the new facility. If he did, we could give him a newbie and he would be a great mentor. Guess I'd better let Trevor talk to him about that. He does like to follow chain of command and protocol. Being in the military will do that to you, I suspect. Maybe he was anal before he went on active duty and is just more so, now. Ah*

74

the questions inquiring minds of corporate VPs can create.

Charles was walking across the parking lot when he heard, "Hey Chaplain, got a minute?" *Crap, it's never just a minute and I really don't want to hear any more problems, today.* "Sure, what can I do to be useful to you?" he said turning to see the familiar face of a Registered Nurse and former counseling client.

CHAPTER 6

"Let's get started," said Bill Groene, FACHE, CEO of MMHS. "The Budget Review Committee is now called to order. Chaplain, thanks for being here. What would you like to tell us about Pastoral Care Services?"

"Good afternoon, everyone. I am quite aware we are asking for a seven percent total increase in our 2006 budget and the guidance was 'Not more than four percent.' I would call to your attention that Pastoral Care Services offset our 2005 operating expenses by 27% or $442,696. That is an increase of two percentage points over the FY 04 offset results of 25%. What is not reflected in the proposed budget is that we have documentable evidence of no less than three law suits against the System being averted by PCS chaplains. We have not added that to the cost avoidance column in the FY '06 budget."

"Chaplain, you can't document what didn't happen" challenged Carmen Lopez, MHA, CEO of Metro Methodist, Central Methodist and Cibolo Methodist hospitals. Because they were all adjacent to the I-35 corridor from downtown San Antonio to the northern most community of Bexar County, they were referred to, simply, as the Corridor hospitals.

"That's true, Carmen. What we **can** document is that a nurse noticed a woman who was behaving strangely outside the nursery at Mercy Methodist, and called the duty chaplain. He engaged her in conversation and she shared with him she had delivered a stillborn child at Mercy three months before this incident and 'That she was there to steal a baby to take home with her.' After getting her permission to tell the nurse so that they could get her the help she needed, Chaplain Gustafson alerted security, went with her and security to the Specialty Hospital and stayed with her until she was admitted to Six East, the inpatient psych unit. Dr. Jamison diagnosed her as having an acute psychotic break as a result of unresolved post partum depression. How much do you think a stolen infant would have cost us? At least five times my total budget."

"The other two situations were less dramatic, but the families were threatening law suit for improper care of their loved one and after a chaplain was called in to hear their complaints and get resolution of them, the threats went away. We all know that most law suits are not for malpractice. They are for poor customer service and/or unresolved control needs. I can't prove those families would have sued, but if I was only half right, and only one family hired a lawyer, PCS saved the System a boat load of money."

"Wait a minute, Chaplain. You lost me on that one. What do you mean unresolved control needs?" asked Charlotte Wiggins, the comptroller.

"If families can't control the fact that Momma is dying, they compensate, usually at an unconscious level, by trying to control other things in their environment—like suing the britches off the hospital if Momma's meds are late. Not that that would have any impact on the outcome of her case if she is terminally ill."

"I once had a patient," continued Charles, "who was on the critical list as a result of an MVA. We weren't sure she was going to make it. Her adult daughter came into the ICU one day and ripped off the face of the charge nurse because the staff hadn't continued to put petroleum jelly on Mom's feet as the daughter had told them. Mom had chronically dry feet. The daughter was trying to control what she could because she couldn't control what was scaring the bejeesus out of her. We see it all the time."

Several were nodding their heads in consensus, including Helen Parker, Chief Nursing Executive. She had been at Mercy Methodist since

God was a little boy and had the power to prove it. Her staff loved her because she had fought hard for them, regardless the issue, and had protected them when doctors or administrators were being less than kind. If she agreed with you, you were golden. And right then, Charles T. McRae, D. Min., BCC, LPC, VP for Pastoral Care Services was golden.

The conversation quickly digressed into chasing rabbits until Bill Groene brought the group back to the agenda at hand. "Chaplain, would you mind continuing?" Bill asked

"You will also note that in the revenue column, we generated $275,096, or 16.8% of our operating expenses."

"How did you do that?" asked the Reverend Wilem T. Torrington, M. Div., chair of the Board of Governors of the System.

Charles suppressed a smile as his friend and advocate asked a question to which he already knew the answer. He was a master at "playing dumb" to reveal information he thought germane to the conversation. He had been Charles' "Straight man" a number of times. Bill Groene was less successful in suppressing his amusement.

"Page three of the PCS budget shows the revenue and cost avoidance for last year. We generated $150,596 with the Pastoral Counseling Center..."

"Isn't that the outpatient portion of our psych services?" Wilem asked, innocently.

"Yes, sir, it is. We also generated $54,500 in consulting fees."

"What kind of consulting do you do?" asked Carmen.

"Well, we generated $7,500 in a five day training we did for the Air Force on Trauma Ministry, $6000 for the training we did for BAMC (Brooke Army Medical Center) and $3,400 on the two Pastoral Care 101 courses we held for local clergy. We were asked by three District Superintendents (of the SWTC) to consult with churches that were in destructive conflict. Out of the four gigs, we generated $19,600. We generated $3,000 when Dr. Trevor Conyers and I did a crisis intervention at First Church in San Antonio. The Bishop asked us to work with the staff and key leaders when the senior pastor resigned his pulpit and came out of the closet. Ted Anglemeyer, Director of the Pastoral Counseling Center, made two trips to Kentucky to help an independent psych hospital develop an IOP (Intensive Outpatient) program for soldiers with acute PTSD who have returned from Iraq or Afghanistan. That made us $15,000. FYI, we will be going back to Kentucky three times in this FY and are negotiating with Ft. Lewis, Washington, Walter Reed Army Medical Center and Ft. Lee, Virginia for this year. Hiring retired and former military chaplains with the skill sets of Clinical Chaplains and Behavioral Health providers is a real advantage."

"You're saying that farming out your chaplains as consultants and trainers generates hard dollars for the System?" asked Carmen. "I never knew that. Do they do this in addition to their regular duties or in lieu of them?"

"They do it on company time and the revenue they produce comes to us. If they do something on their own vacation time or FTO (flexible time off), they keep the money," replied Charles. "We do the same thing with the chaplains who have credentials as psychotherapist by having them carry a small case load in the Counseling Center and in doing in-services, workshops, training and consulting in their areas of expertise."

"Dr. Anglemeyer does quite a bit of training, both internally for in-services and externally for the Behavioral Health Community. He also teaches a course in Family Systems Theory at Our Lady of the Lake University on his own time that generates no hard dollars for us, but it does give some referrals to the PCC as well as a lot of good will with the University. Additionally, he is always in demand in the hinterlands of South Texas. It's much more cost effective to send him there, than expect a group to come here. By doing that, we're not in competition with the glut of behavioral health types in the San Antonio, Austin area to provide CEUs (Continuing Education Units). This year he generated $68,500, which is more than his annual salary."

"We, of course, offer our Brown Bag Seminars at Methodist Specialty Hospital to provide super cheap CEUs that they all need to stay licensed. That created $1,500. We bring in someone once a quarter to talk about the System's continuum of care in Behavioral Health, thereby getting more referrals for inpatient, Intensive Out Patient, Partial Day and the other psych programs we offer. It's a win-win for our allies in the community."

"How do you cover their duties when they are consulting?" asked Carmen.

"The same way Nursing, RT, PT or Nutrition Services covers when people are sick, on FMLA (Family Medical Leave Act), or vacation. We have a chaplain carrying the duty pager 24x7 in the Medical Center, in house and one for the Corridor, out of house. As you know, we also have a third chaplain carrying the SAFE pager, out of house, separately from the duty chaplain responsibilities. They both do a lot of the back up when chaplains are gone through the day, and when necessary, we use pool chaplains to maintain our established policies on coverage ratios and standards of care," Charles said softly as he waited for the trap to spring.

"So if we did away with all this consulting and the additional expense of using the pool, we could reduce the number of FTEs in your department, thus saving money," Carmen said with a smug grin. "Why don't we just stick to core functions and do away with all these bells and whistles?"

"We could," said Charles. Carmen's grin got bigger. "Or, we could increase our efforts in consulting, generate more revenue and have an even greater impact on our sphere of influence in the seventeen county catchment area, thus producing more outpatient migration from the rural, community and regional hospitals. That produces more revenue and volume for the System. It also builds relationships with our colleagues 'out there.' Taylor and I have both had gigs helping medical groups, nursing staffs and boards resolve conflict. In addition to swaying their out migration to us, it helps them know more about how Clinical Chaplaincy can be a 'value added' rather than a revenue drain. As Johnny Jones can attest, we have been able to place four chaplains, three full time and one part time, in the rural areas. When Johnny is talking to the CEOs and boards about signing a management agreement with MMHS, part of each package is a free

Pastoral Care needs assessment done by me or one of our directors. We've also done some training of the local ministerial alliances who provide volunteer pastoral care to the staff and patients of their local hospitals, usually, gratis."

"One of our core functions, as defined in our 2010 Strategic Plan, is to grow PCS as a resource to the facilities I just mentioned and lead our competition in services provided outside of San Antonio." Carmen's smile faded into a furrowed brow. Charles added, "By being the only Level I (the highest) Pastoral Care System in the state and all of HSI, we generate more and better economies of scale through hiring only the best chaplains who are double and triple credentialed, thereby being able to get more services, and revenue out of them—when we're not dealing with staff, patients and families."

"I thought that the patient always comes first. They're the customer," said Carmen, indignantly.

"That's correct, Carmen, the patients are the System's customers. It's been my experience, and that of the majority of our chaplains, that if we take care of the staff, they will take care of us in terms of where and how we need to be spending our time. They tell us which patients need to be seen, who's upset or has gotten bad news and which families are struggling or growing hostile. Together we can do a better job of taking care of patients and families thus improving patient and family satisfaction. It's also important that they know we are there for them and give them opportunities to vent or grieve when they're having a bad day. Think of it as the informal and preventative arm of the Employee Assistance Program."

"As you know, it is not our goal to see every patient, every day. It's our goal to spend our time where we are needed most and avoid doing 'roller skate ministry.' We have Chapel Volunteers and Special Ministers of the Eucharist, for the Catholics, to do that. By design, we are the work place pastors of our 6800 employees. If they're having a bad day with a supervisor, colleague, patient or family, they don't usually call the pastor of the church they attend. They call us because of the rapport we have already established through our time on the units and interactions in every

81

place from the cafeteria to the class room. We're there to serve them and they pick up on that quickly." Charles paused to see if Carmen or anyone else had more questions.

"In the cost avoidance column on the same page you see that our internal Employee Assistance Program saves the system $163,000 a year and we did 46 hours of in-services, which, at $100 an hour, the minimum we would pay to bring in someone, we saved the System $4,600."

"That's impressive, Chaplain," volunteered Helen. No one challenged her.

"I would like to add one more point to the discussion. As ya'll know, it costs, on average, $10,000 to recruit one nurse. Retention is the name of the cost savings game and we are an integral part of the employee retention program. Last year over twenty nurses gave PCS chaplains credit for helping them choose to stay with MMHS," Charles said. He then sat quietly as he looked around the room. Helen Parker was, again, nodding consent.

"I move we approve the PCS budget as presented," said The Reverend Wilem T. Torrington. Helen Parker seconded. There was no discussion and the budget was passed, unanimously.

Charles got up to leave, and Bill Groene said, "Let's take a ten minute break before we review the Marketing Budget." There were no arguments.

06/1615 January 2006

"Nice job in there," said Bill Groene as he and Charles walked out of the conference room.

"Thanks", said Charles. "I was sweating bullets before the meeting. I don't do a good job of keeping all that information straight in a presentation like this one. My fear is I'll screw up and we'll have to cut staff. That's one of my least favorite things to do."

"And mine," replied Bill. "I really regret that we didn't get the budget approved before JACHO hit last October. There's only so much time in the day. By the way, we skipped right over what an SIT program is. Why don't I give you some time at our next Senior Leaders' Meeting to present that? I really like what you're doing with PCS. Keep it up."

"Thanks, Bill. That means a lot. Good luck with the rest of the budget review work." Charles walked away without his feet touching the ground. He was elated. Bill rarely gave outright compliments and was never effusive. A "Good Job" from him was like a five minute recitation of affirmation from the Bishop. Credibility and understanding of Clinical Chaplaincy was always an issue and a continuing task of education with the rest of the staff. Quantifying successful ministry was also an ongoing challenge. But today, at least for a little while, he was very pleased. And he would enjoy it for as long as it lasted, knowing that tomorrow, there would be more dragons to slay and crises to manage. It was his reality and he usually dealt with it pretty well. *Can't wait to tell Beth. Maybe dinner at Pasta Vino would be in order.*

06/1618 January 2006

Charles' pager vibrated on his belt. He read the script as it scrolled across the micro screen, "Ethics consult at 1700, 7E." *That didn't take long*, he thought to himself. And there goes a quiet dinner with Beth. Four minutes later, he walked into the PCS System suite of offices. Anna Travers greeted him with a smile and, "Did you get the page?"

"Yes, I did. Do you know what it's about?"

"I'm not sure. Mara O'Reilly called and said they had a problem patient on MICU."

"Imagine that. And it's so important we have to do it, today?" asked Charles, rhetorically. Anna shrugged and smiled as the phone rang.

"Pastoral Care Services," she replied with a smile in her voice.

Damn she's good, especially for this time of day, thought Charles. *Hope some of that wears off on Sarah.* He frequently wondered, in an unkind way, how Sarah got across the street in the morning without getting run over. He had delegated her hiring to Anna, Sister Joyce and Tom Clarke, Chief Resident, because she would be admin support to the CPE program and supervised by Joyce.

Sarah presented well and came highly recommended from her former employer. She had great computer skills and no common sense. *Who knew?*

06/1700 January 2006

The usual suspects sat around the table in the nurses' lounge, except for a young female physician Charles didn't recognize. He greeted the others and then introduced himself to Janice A. Murray, MD. She was the reason the ethics consultation team had been called into session. Missy Troyer, RN, MSN called the meeting to order. She was the convener of the team for Mercy Methodist. The other member was Camryn Roth, MD. Each of the hospitals had a three person ethics team that tried to resolve the issues before calling for the ten to fifteen member ethics committee to meet.

"Let's get started," said Missy. "Dr. Murray has requested the three of us meet to discuss a patient she is having problems with. Guillermo Sanchez is a fifty-seven year old Hispanic male in end-stage renal failure due to Type 2 diabetes. He is also in multiple systems failure and will probably not leave the hospital, alive. He knows he is dying and wants to go home, but the family wants to do everything possible. A secondary problem is that he and his family are noncompliant with his dietary plan. They sneak in chips, salsa, candy and other inappropriate foods every time they visit, which is daily. The dietician and Dr. Murray have both talked to them and the patient. Their English is limited and nothing, so far, has gotten them to change their behavior. It's very frustrating for Dr. Murray and the staff."

"I am at my wits end," announced Dr. Murray. "I have tried everything I know to do and nothing is working. They just keep bringing Mr. Sanchez the stuff he likes. He complains about the hospital food and doesn't eat it. The family wants me to do everything possible, but then they sabotage the treatment plan. I just don't know what to do."

"Have you talked with the family about the fact Mr. Sanchez is actively dying?" asked Charles.

"Yes I have," said Dr. Murray. "They seem to understand that. But then they keep bringing in his wife's food and other things. It's very frustrating."

"Sounds like you're feeling pretty helpless," added Charles.

"Yes I am. I just started my practice in San Antonio a few months ago and this case is taking so much of my time. They are all sweet people, but they won't do what I tell them they need to do for the patient."

"I think we need to tell them that if they don't comply, we can't provide the heroic measures they want," said Dr. Roth. "We can't be wasting resources if they aren't going to do their part."

"I think we may have some communication and cultural problems," said Charles. "I'd like to call in Father Gonzalez. He's an old style priest from Spain, of late Mexico, and I think he may be able to help." Missy, and the doctors nodded assent. Charles called his office and asked Anna to page Father Gonzalez to MICU. Three minutes later the good Padre arrived, looking as confused as ever.

Charles stepped out of the nurses' lounge and briefed the aging priest, who was soon to celebrate his eightieth birthday, on the situation. He walked into the glass cubicle and began talking with the patient and family. A few minutes later, he anointed the patient, hugged the wife and daughters and walked across the unit to where the team sat ensconced in banal conversation in the lounge.

Father spoke in his broken English to tell the *Gringos* gathered that both the patient and the family know he is dying but that culturally it is disrespectful to discuss this with each other. He said Mr. Sanchez was able to say he just wanted to go home, enjoy his wife's cooking and be with his family until he died. The family was quite relieved and agreed to his plan.

Charles thanked the good Father for his help, all ten minutes of it, and looked at the others in the room as the priest left. "I think we have a plan," he said. The others agreed and the meeting ended. *It's all about communication and realizing we're not here to get OUR needs met. What a waste of time. Maybe Beth and I can go out to dinner, after all.*

CHAPTER 7

09/0830 January 2006

"Good morning, all," said Sister Joyce O'Reilly, CDP, BCC. The six chaplain residents momentarily stopped their munching on donuts, jelly rolls and bear claws brought by Tom Clarke, M. Div., Chief Resident (Read: Second year).

"Good Morning, Sister," the residents chimed, bringing a smile to Joyce's face. She flashed back twenty-five years to when she was a sixth grade teacher at St. Jerome's Church and School in her native Kentucky. The ritual never changed.

"Let's get started," she said. Checking her notes, she said, "I see Anthony is up for presenting his verbatim. What do you have for us, Anthony?" she asked innocently. Tony Pena, M. Div., was a third generation Italian American from Trenton, New Jersey. He was considered handsome by most, was light hearted and had a quick wit. He was well liked by his colleagues and the staff. When he graduated from High School in 1996, he packed his '92 Camero and headed to Ft. Worth, Texas where he matriculated at Texas Christian University. It was the furthest school he could find from New Jersey and his dysfunctional family.

After graduating from TCU with a BA in History, he enrolled in Brite Divinity School, across University Boulevard from the undergraduate school. He was in the Army R.O.T.C. program while in college and was commissioned a Second Lieutenant of Infantry in the U.S. Army. He applied for and received an educational delay to attend graduate school. His goal was to be an Army chaplain. He genuinely hoped that the wars in Iraq and Afghanistan would not be over before he accessioned to active duty. His year of CPE was necessary to be endorsed by the Christian, Disciples of Christ, Church and to become a Military Chaplain. He was married to Carol Ann, daughter of a west Texas Oilman. They met during their sophomore year at TCU.

Tony began handing Sister and his colleagues copies of his verbatim with no little anxiety. He hated doing verbatims. They were the bane of all CPE students. They were required to prepare as exact a replication of a conversation they had with a patient, family member or staff member, as memory made possible. That was prefaced with the location, time, and events leading to the documented interchange. They also had to give a theological reflection of the conversation identifying what significant issues were presented and then ascertain how appropriately they responded to the other person.

The verbatim was then presented to the other residents and their supervisor, Sister Joyce. It was a way to hone their pastoral skills, she had explained. It was also an exercise in humility and character building as each person took their turn suggesting where he had erred and/or how he could have done it better. Sister Joyce always went last. By the time she spoke, the blood was flowing, metaphorically speaking. Under the best of circumstances, there was always something missed or that could have been done better. Today was somewhere between bad and awful.

The situation recorded took place in the nurses' station of the SICU around 0300 a day earlier. Tony was on call and had just "handled" a death. As he had been taught, he then made rounds through the ICUs of Mercy Methodist to see what other crises awaited him. As he sat, sipping a cup of coffee, one of the nurses began chatting with him. She was just a little younger than he and was dating one of the physician residents. She wanted to get married and the good doctor wasn't grasping her not-so-subtle hints.

The nurse began to tell Tony of her frustrations. In the verbatim, as in the actual conversation, he changed the subject. A moment later, she returned to the topic of her relationship and, again, Tony changed the subject. This happened several times before the nurse left to attend a patient. Tony finished his rounds and went back to the office to await the next crisis.

"You kept blocking her attempts to engage you," said Sandy.

"No I didn't. We were just talking. She wasn't trying to have an informal counseling session," replied Tony a little more defensively than intended.

"I think I would have been really pissed if I were her," said Nicole Patrick, RN, M.Div. "She gave you every lead in the book to be her confidant and you closed the door on her. You did, really."

"I didn't mean to. I was just chatting with her while I rested and drank my coffee."

"Why do you suppose you missed the cues, Anthony?" asked Sister Joyce in a kind voice.

"I guess I was a little tired and I was still thinking about the death I had just handled. The guy was only fifty-four and had had a routine bowel resection due to diverticulitis. He wasn't supposed to die. His wife, now widow, is the same age as my mom."

"A little?" asked Joyce.

"Maybe it was more like I was exhausted," Tony thought out loud.

"Sounds like you were also experiencing some temporary compassion fatigue and transference," added Sister Joyce. "It's no wonder. How old is your dad?"

"He's fifty-three and mom is forty-nine. Guess it was just too close to home."

"Sounds like coaching someone in how to seduce her boyfriend into marriage wasn't real high on your priority list," said Tom Clarke. "Happens to the best of us. Last year I came home from a really hard day. I had been duty chaplain and had two deaths and a code. It was my weekend with the kids and my fifteen year old daughter went drama queen over a broken finger nail. I just really didn't give a shit and she knew it. Later I

89

felt like a jerk because I realized her problem was a real one for her. Sometimes it really blows me away how different our days are to the average public. Even to other clergy."

"I, we, handle more death and trauma in a week than I did in a year when I was in the local church. It's just a totally different world here." Everyone was nodding in agreement. "When I was in the local church, I averaged about a funeral a month. Most of the people who died were in their eighties, or even nineties. In some cases, it was a blessing. Sure not what we see here," said Sandy. There was more nodding.

"So, Anthony, tell us how you could have done things differently?" said Sister Joyce.

"I guess I should have paid more attention to her," said Tony.

"I'm not sure that was realistic. You were physically and emotionally exhausted," said Joyce.

"Maybe I should have gone up to the office to rest before making rounds. Maybe logging in the death would have helped. I don't know. I didn't necessarily want to be by myself, but I didn't want to do any counseling either."

"Sounds like you were looking for someone to nurture you. That's normal enough," said John Wilson. "Can't fault you for that, except that few of the staff see us as the ones who need nurturing. We're supposed to be there for them. It's a bit of a sticky wicket, as it were."

"It's embarrassing to admit that I was looking for caring, rather than trying to give it," said Tony.

"Is this nurse attractive?" asked Sister.

Tony blushed and began to stammer. He took a deep breath and said, "She's extremely pretty and to be honest I have a bit of a crush on her, or at least I have some attraction to her."

"That's courageous of you to share that with your peers, Anthony," said Sister Joyce. "It's totally normal. It's also one of the hazards of the job. I assume that there is a great deal of sex going on among the staff."

"Yeah, I walked in on a doctor and a nurse doing it in one of the empty patient rooms the other night when I was on call," said Nicole with a conspiratorial tone in her voice.

"I can name at least six married staff who are having affairs with someone they work with. This hospital is its own little soap opera," added Sandy. "Sometimes I just can't believe it."

"Why do you suppose that is?" the residents' supervisor asked rhetorically. "It's called trauma bonding. When one deals with life and death issues, it increases all the appetites. I assume you are aware of the number of firefighters who fell in love with their colleagues' widows after 9-11? There is something about going through a crisis with someone that is seductive, for both. Don't think because you are clergy that you are not subject to that dynamic. In some ways, you are more susceptible."

"Why is that Sister," asked Tony. "In my denomination, when a guy is ordained, his balls fall off!" The group laughed heartily as some of the anxiety in the group slipped away.

"Oh that that were so," said Sandy. Clergy **MEN** are the worst when it comes to dating. They're as horny as a six peckered Billy goat, as we say in South Texas." She was smiling as she said it and then glanced at Sister Joyce to see how she was handling the conversation. She was smiling as were all the students.

"You don't remember your Bible very well," said Joyce in mock chastisement. "Remember The Fall? That's the story where Eve got framed. Forbidden fruit is always sweeter. The Church in general has done a poor job of dealing with human sexuality, either theologically or ethically. "Just Say No," has never been a successful marketing campaign. It actually increases the appetite. And that's a word of warning to you all. On that note, we're out of time. Be sure you finish reading the book I assigned last week before tomorrow's didactic seminar."

Sister Joyce walked out of the room leaving her students in stunned silence as they reflected on their own experiences—especially the ones they thought only they had had.

Oh my God! Why did I just think of Dr. Smarty pants? thought Sandy. *Like I need to be involved with him.* As she exited the conference room, a mental image of Karl T. Sassmann, MD, naked, lying on a sleep room cot, invaded her mind. She was horrified, blushed and ducked into the women's room to hide in a stall until she thought she had control of herself. She felt slightly nauseous as she walked back into the hallway.

09/1100 January 2006

"Burn team to ABICU, burn team to ABICU," squawked the overhead public address system.

Crap! thought Tony. He had just walked into the cafeteria for lunch when he heard the announcement. He was duty chaplain and had to handle the new burn case. He was tired from the verbatim conference and hungry. He turned on his heel and headed to the Adult Burn ICU.

As he walked to the table next to the exterior of the door to the assessment room to don his sterile gown, mask, hair net, gloves and booties, he saw Leslie Carr, RN, MSN, head nurse of the Adult Burn ICU. "What do we have?" he asked much more casually than he felt.

"Twenty-five year old Caucasian female burned with boiling water when she slipped on her kitchen floor, knocking a pot off the stove and onto herself."

"Do you know the percent of burn?" asked Tony.

"No Chaplain, that's why she's in the assessment room."

"Touché. May I ask you something? This is the first time I've worked a case with a **young** woman. Chaplain Thomas has taught us that we are supposed to go into the shower room with the patient when they are being debrided and assessed. Do you think she is going to be upset with me seeing her naked?"

"I don't know. Why don't you ask her?"

"Touché, again. I just want you to know that I don't feel as stupid as I act," said Tony smiling.

"That's a good thing," said Leslie, smiling behind her mask as she entered the assessment room.

Tony entered the room just behind her, pulling his surgical mask over his nose and mouth. He walked to the head of the patient and began the trauma protocol he had learned a lifetime ago. *Okay, so it was just six months, but it seems a lot longer than that. I wonder what she's going to say about me being with her during the debridement?* At that moment, the Medical Resident doing the initial exam from the other side of the gurney told the patient he wanted her to sit up. As he assisted her by placing his hand on her back, the sheet covering her naked body fell into her lap. Tony felt a stirring in his loins as he gazed upon a pair of magnificent breasts. *Thank God I'm wearing a gown* he thought to himself. The patient, Cindy Campbell, was completely unfazed by the event. The Chaplain (Resident) began to regain his composure and was able to make eye contact with the patient. Again, Leslie smiled behind her mask as she watched the interchange.

09/1330 January 2006

"For a 'Baby Chaplain,' you did a good job in there," said Leslie as the team was taking off their sterile garb. Cindy had been moved to a cubicle in the ABICU and Leslie and Tony were going out to talk to the family. He would then bring them into the unit to see Cindy, as per the protocol.

"I guess that's a compliment, or at least I choose to take it that way," said Tony, exuding his natural charm. He knew Leslie was several years older than he, but she was good looking and liked to flirt. He was willing to oblige her and respond in kind. He knew the term "Baby Chaplain" was what some of the staff called the residents as a sign of affection and not so subtle reminder of their place in the food chain.

Leslie wrapped on the door to the family room just down the corridor from the ABICU, as she walked through it. A couple was sitting on the love seat. The man had his arm around the woman, who had been crying. They were dressed in noticeably expensive, casual clothes. *He was obviously on the golf course when he got the call. I'll bet she was at the mall, no doubt at Nordstrom*, thought Tony a bit unkindly. "*Being judgmental gets in the way of your ministry,*" Tony heard Sister Joyce's voice say. *No doubt I'm just a tad bit envious*, thought Tony. *Hey, I just "self-supervised."* Tony was quite proud of himself for performing a Level II CPE function. *Can't wait to tell Sister Joyce.* Leslie's voice broke into Tony's revelry.

"Mr. and Mrs. Holzman?" asked Leslie.

"Yes," the man said. "And this is Dan Campbell, Cindy's husband," nodding toward the young man sitting in a chair against the wall the door was on. Tony hadn't noticed him. *He looks like he'd fall over if I blew on him, thought Tony. How did a wimp like him get a fine looking woman like Cindy? Oops, there I go being judgmental again. Damn.*

"I'm Leslie Carr, Nurse Manager for the ABICU and this is Chaplain Tony Pena. We have been with Cindy during her assessment and treatment. Her vital signs are stable and she tolerated the initial procedures well. She's in a bed in her cubicle and Chaplain Pena will take you in to see her in a few minutes. Dr. Weisman is completing his assessment and will tell you about the extent of her injuries while you are with her. I'll be talking with you after that about some of our policies and suggestions for being supportive of Cindy during and after her hospitalization.

She was primarily talking to Dan Campbell, because he was the Next of Kin, which seemed to be annoying Mr. Holzman. "Has Cindy ever been hospitalized before?" she asked Dan.

"She has had fourteen surgeries in her young life due to a congenital anomaly in her right ankle," said Mr. Holzman, before Dan, who had the proverbial 'Deer in the headlights' stare, could respond. She's been through a lot. I guess that's why she has such a high pain threshold," Holzman continued.

"I noticed that," said Leslie. "She really is quite brave. That will help her a lot while she's here and going through rehab."

It also explains why she was not concerned about being nude in front of several men, thought Tony. *I guess that was helpful to me, too.*

"How long have you and Cindy been married?" asked Leslie.

"Uh, about a year," said Dan.

94

"Actually, it's been almost fourteen months. They were married November 19, 2004," added Mr. Holzman. Mrs. Holzman rolled her eyes and mimed the word "Sorry" to the others in the room without her husband seeing her. Tony and Leslie suppressed smiles and avoided looking at each other. Dan still had the thousand-yard stare.

"I'm going to leave you in Chaplain Pena's good care," said Leslie, "As I said before, he will go with you to see Cindy." She immediately exited before anyone could ask any questions. Her pager had vibrated several times while she was in the family room. To her credit, thought Tony, she had not looked at it once.

"I just want to prepare you for how Cindy is going to look when we go in to see her," said Tony. "She will be rather different from the last time you were with her. The burns occurred primarily on her left side, with a few small 'splash burns' on her abdomen and chest. The left side of her face is somewhat swollen as is her left arm. They have placed a nasogastric tube in her nose that goes down to her stomach." He saw the look of confusion on Dan's face and added, "It helps to keep her from throwing up. She has IVs in both hands and a nasal cannula for oxygen to help her breathe and keep her O2 sats up."

"What's that mean?" asked Dan.

"I'm sorry," said Tony. "That means she will have a small plastic tube across her face with two small extensions that go just inside her nostrils. By giving her additional oxygen, it will help her have a higher percentage of oxygen in her blood stream, hence faster healing, and more O2 to the brain. She has an IV in the back of each hand. She has a Foley catheter so she can void her bladder without getting out of bed and they can measure her output."

"This is all standard procedure for someone in her situation. It's not anything to be alarmed about," said Tony with a reassuring tone. "She will also have a white cream on the burns. Also," he paused to look at each of them to ensure they were ready for the next piece on information. When they were all looking at him, he said, "We practice an open wound system in which the patients have neither bandages nor clothes. She will

95

have some gauze over her breasts and pubic area." He paused to let that sink in.

"I encourage you to touch her where she is not burned. Our patients all feel pretty unattractive and touching them communicates your love and acceptance at a basic level. Please don't pat her. Just lay your hand on a shoulder, hand or knee. Our former patients have told us it is disconcerting when people pat them."

"Won't it hurt her if we touch her?" asked Mr. Holzman.

"Not unless you touch her wounds. Any place where she doesn't have the white cream is okay," said Tony.

"Is she in pain?" asked Mrs. Holzman.

Tony paused for a moment as he decided how to answer the question. "She will probably be experiencing some pain...."

"Then why in the hell aren't they giving her medication to stop it. When I had by-pass surgery last year, they kept me snowed the whole time. I didn't feel anything the first few days," said Mr. Holzman, rather indignantly.

"I assume you were on a vent, er I mean a respirator following surgery?"

"For the first two days" said Mr. Holzman.

"Cindy is not on a respirator, and if we give her enough pain medication to eradicate it all, it will also stop her breathing. Obviously, we don't want to do that." The couple nodded in unison. Dan continued to have "the stare." Clearly, he was not present emotionally or cognitively. He continued to have it as Tony reached over and gently placed his hand on Dan's shoulder. He looked down as, for the first time, tears began to run down his cheeks.

After a moment of silence, with no little fidgeting on the part of Mr. H, he started to say something. The "baby chaplain" gently raised his open hand in the direction of Holzman and waited until he lowered his head, remaining silent. *I'll be damned. It worked*, thought Tony. Chaplain Trevor Conyers, D. Min., LPC, LMFT, BCC, Director of Clinical Chaplaincy Services had taught them that during a didactic session along with

96

many other helpful techniques for relating to family members and patients. Tony asked, after another two minutes of silence and considerable squirming by *Holzman*, as Tony began to think of him, "Are you ready?" They all nodded. "I'll be right back. I want to make sure she's ready for us to visit her." He didn't wait for a response as he silently slipped out of the room. He hurried down the hall to Cindy's glass cubicle. The nurse assigned to her and one other patient quickly stopped what she was doing and nodded with a brief smile from behind her mask, communicating Cindy was ready to receive her family. Chaplain (Resident) Anthony Pena, M. Div. in his most professional manner, assessed the situation and then returned to the family room. He wrapped lightly as he opened the door. "She's ready. Let's go. She looks pretty much as I described her. This will be hard. Just do the best you can and if you need to express feelings, try to wait until we get back here to express them. We want to be positive and supportive of her. Any questions?" There were none. He held the door open for the family and then led them down the hallway.

At the small table a few feet from the first cubicle, he stopped and patiently explained to them how to put on the sterile gown, booties, hair net, mask and finally gloves. After a few frustrating attempts, Dan got all his fingers in the right parts of the gloves. Mr. H made no attempt to hide his impatience or contempt.

"Cindy. I have some folks who want to see you. They'll look a little funny with all the stuff on, but you'll recognize them," said Tony in a forced, cheerful tone. He stepped away from the bed and strategically placed himself behind Mrs. H and Dan who were on the same side of the bed. Mr. H was on the other side taking it all in with a rather critical countenance.

Dad took charge. *No surprise there*, thought Tony, and began with a few words of encouragement. He then began to pepper her with questions about what happened, why the pot handle wasn't over the stove instead of over the floor, why there was water on the floor before the accident, why she didn't see it and then "teased" her about being her usual clumsy self.

Very nice, asshole was Tony's thought as heard himself say, "I think that's enough for now. We need to let Cindy rest. Mrs. Holzman, do you have anything you would like to say before we go?"

"We love you Cindy and want you to get well really soon. We're just down the hall if you need us," she said as she turned to leave. Her eyes were moist.

"Is there anything you want to tell your daughter?" asked Tony.

Mr. H seemed shocked at the question. He cleared his throat, tried to form words and then said, gruffly, "Love you," as he turned to exit Cindy's room. He was ashen and unsure of his steps.

Mrs. H had walked a few steps past the last cubicle, leaned against the wall and broke into heavy sobs as she bent over double. Tony noticed all this out of the corner of his eye. Mr. Holzman seemed oblivious to his wife. Dan Campbell seemed okay for the moment, so Tony walked briskly to her. He gently laid his arm across her shoulders and pulled her into his lower chest. She continued to sob a few more moments. In time, she caught her breath, stood erect and began to wipe her face with a tissue. She took a deep breath and looked at Tony as if to say, "Now what?"

"Mrs. Holzman, I'm …."

"Please call me Jean. After that display of emotion, formality seems a bit inappropriate."

"Jean, I know this is extremely painful for you. I just want you to know I care. Would you like to go back to the family room?" She nodded and began to walk in that direction. Tony went with her as he motioned to Mr. H, who began to walk over in his zombiesque manner. "Sir, I think it would be a good idea if you went with your wife to the family room. I'm going to check on Dan and then I'll be right there."

The man looked ten years older than he had in the family room, as he made his way down the corridor. They were the image of despair. Hope was a concept that had been radically ripped from their lexicon of life.

Dan Campbell was standing next to his wife's bed with a look of total hopelessness. His psychic transport from life had placed him in a world more foreign than Mars. He stared first at one beeping machine and then another. He watched the IV line drip its antibiotic laden solution into Cindy's body. He could assign no meaning to his surreal experience.

"This must seem totally unreal for you," Tony said as he gently laid his hand on Dan's shoulder. The young husband crumpled to the floor as if an anvil had fallen on him. Tony knelt on one knee as he reached around Dan's shoulders and pulled him to himself. He noticed a nurse peering through the glass wall as her raised eyebrows portrayed curiosity and concern. Tony nodded to say "He's okay." The nurse wandered on to other duties.

After a few moments of heavy sobbing, Dan began to recover his composure and started trying to stand. He was as unsteady as a new born foal. Tony had to help him get his balance and then stand. He looked at Cindy as one studies an insect or strange formation of lichen. Slowly, recognition seeped into his eyes. He hesitantly reached to touch his wife's bare shoulder. She turned her head slightly in the direction of the tactile stimulation and opened her eyes. "I'm so sorry." Sobs returned as his knees weakened. Tony was ready to catch him, but he was able to keep his balance. "I'm so sorry, Cindy. I was so angry at you. I just left it so you'd have to clean it. I never thought this would happen. I'm so sorry, so, so sorry."

"Remind her what you were angry about," said Tony in a soothing voice.

Dan looked at the chaplain and confessed, "We had just had a fight over something, I can't even remember what. It was stupid, something inconsequential. I was still pissed at her when I spilled some water next to the stove and deliberately didn't clean it up. I went to my study and a few minutes later heard Cindy scream. I found her lying on the floor next to the stove with water all around her. I didn't know what to do. She had to tell me to call 911. I was just frozen. When I saw what had happened, I knew immediately it was my fault. How can she ever forgive me?"

Tony waited a minute before responding. "If you had known this would happen, would you have cleaned up the spill?"

"Of course I would have."

"But you didn't know that, did you? If you knew that you would have a major traffic accident going home the usual way, do you think you might try an alternate route?" asked Tony.

"Yes, but how would I know that?" replied Dan.

"Precisely my point, Dan. You wouldn't, any more than if you knew Cindy would slip, fall and knock the pan of boiling water on her. By the way, was she still angry at you?"

"Yeah, I guess so. I just wish this hadn't happened. She's already had so much to endure. Do you think she will ever be able to forgive me?"

"I don't know, why don't you ask her?" Tony said as he nodded toward the bed. *Score one for the kid and Leslie. Guess I'm a quick study.*

"*When you finish admiring your pastoral skills, chaplain, you might want to turn your attention to YOUR patient*" Sister Joyce said in Tony's head, jarring him.

"Cindy, I'm so sorry. Please forgive me. I didn't mean to hurt you. I'm so sorry," said Dan in a plaintive voice.

Cindy looked at him and mouthed the words "I forgive you." A tear ran down the side of her face as she closed her eyes. She moved her shoulder ever so slightly to put more pressure against Dan's hand.

"I love you. I love you so much. I'm so sorry. I love you," Dan said again and again.

After a moment of silence, Cindy said faintly with a slight grimace, "I love you, too." She turned her head away from the two men and was immediately asleep feeling the full effects of the pain medication.

Tony gently tugged at Dan's elbow and the two retreated from the room. As they were taking off the sterile precautions, Dan asked, "Why did she grimace when she said I love you. Is she still angry with me?"

"I think the NG tube was irritating the back of her throat. Many patients report that," said Tony in a reassuring tone. *At least I hope that was it. May need to refer them to the Pastoral Counseling Center when she's discharged. A little trauma resolution work and marriage counseling can't hurt.*

CHAPTER 8

10/0738 January 2006

"What's the matter, you couldn't sleep?" asked Charles McRae, D. Min., LPC, BCC; VP for Pastoral Care Services, in mock sincerity of Ted J. Anglemeyer, Psy.D., LPC, LMFT, BCC, Director of the Pastoral Counseling Center, MMHS.

"Nope, tried to, but I kept waking up because the goddamned birds wouldn't shut the fuck up. Decided to come on in and bless this assembled body with my presence," said the Reverend Doctor Anglemeyer. "Damned shame, too. I had nothing to do but attend your silly-assed staff meeting this morning and I would have gladly made the sacrifice of missing that gigantic waste of time for a couple of hours more sleep. I had a client keep me past 5:00 p.m., yesterday. Had to fight traffic all the way around 1604 and out 281, past Bulverde. My cows were getting a bit miffed that I wasn't home on time to feed them."

"As a person of exceptional compassion and empathy, I find it absolutely impossible to offer either," said Charles with a straight face. "Why didn't you just call and ask Princess to feed them?" Everyone burst into laughter. "Sit down and get some vittles and coffee so we can see if it improves your attitude. You're a might more testy than usual this beautiful morning," Charles said in his best Texas twang.

"Beautiful, my ass. It was twenty-eight degrees at my place. Damned near froze to death doing chores. The horses didn't care for it none too much either."

"You know, Ted, I'm never quite sure if you are a psychologist/clergyman who likes to play at being a rancher, or a rancher who plays at being a psychologist/clergyman. Either way, you are one fowl mouthed sumbitch," Said Charles. Sister Joyce just shook her head as she hid her smile by taking another sip of coffee.

"Sister Joyce, I do believe Dr. Anglemeyer's CPE did not 'take' in so much as he continues to use inappropriate language at the breakfast table. Perhaps you should design a remedial course for him and teach him some social graces," said Charles, still smiling.

"As I have told ya'll before, I am not the morality police. Besides, I like a little 'spice' in the conversation now and again. Life at the convent is entirely too boring. I guess I got spoiled all those years I was in Europe as a DRE for the Army."

"I never knew you had been a Director of Religious Education in Germany. Where were you assigned?" asked, Tom Parsons, Psy. D., CEAP, BCC, Director of the Employee Assistance Program, MMHS.

"I was in Kaiserlautern with the 21st Support Command Chaplains' office for five years, eighty to eighty-five. Ted and I were there at the same time, for two years. I left there to do my Supervisor In Training work at Yale Newhaven."

"Yep, Joyce was my spiritual director for over a year. Best one I ever had."

"That's pretty high falutten for a Methodist from Sweetwater, Texas. How in the world did you learn to even spell 'spiritual director?'" asked Charles.

"I was reading a bunch of Andrew Greely's novels during that time and he kept talking about spiritual direction. I had no clue what it was, so one day I asked Joyce. The rest is history, as they say."

"Who's Andrew Greely?" asked Tom.

"He's a Roman Catholic priest with a PhD. in sociology. Use to teach at Arizona State, or was it UofA? Can't remember. Anyway, he wrote <u>Thy Brother's Wife, Ascent Into Hell, Virgin and Martyr</u>, and many more good novels. He also wrote a boat load of Father Blacky mysteries. All the priests are from Chicago. If I ever meet one from there, I swear, I'll feel like his cousin!" said Ted. "He was writing faster than I could read, so I finally quit. The thing that really intrigued me was something he said in his first book, <u>Cardinal Sins</u>. When people asked him why a priest would write a novel in the twentieth century, he replied something to the effect, 'For the same reason a priest in the sixteenth century would create a stained glass window for a church. To share the Gospel.' That made a lot of sense to me. So I just kept reading. He called his first three books the Easter Trilogy. Had some really great theology in them."

Dr. Anglemeyer grew up on a cattle ranch just outside Sweetwater, Texas. He had been called to ministry at the age of twelve, having been a cradle roll member of First Methodist Church, as had his mother, her siblings and her father. His maternal grandmother had been a pillar of the church and was what she described as a "Shouting Methodist." She spoke in tongues (glossolalia) on occasion. Later in the twentieth century that was known as being charismatic. It never really caught on in the Methodist denomination, except in a few local churches.

"Just stating the facts as I see them," said Ted. The waitress had hurried over with a cup of coffee and glass of ice water as soon as she saw him. Charles and his four directors, "The team," met there almost every Tuesday morning at 7:30. He took a pull on his coffee and seemed to settle into his chair a bit more relaxed. With everyone assembled, they ordered their breakfast and talked about how astoundingly cold it was. Anything below thirty-five degrees was considered frigid in South Texas. The 5:00, 6:00 and 10:00 p.m. weather announcers on all the local news programs admonished viewers to remember the "Three Ps of Cold Weather; pets, plants and pipes." Anyone who ever lived north of the Red River, the Oklahoma border with Texas, laughed every time they saw it.

Ted was a long tall drink of water standing 6'2" and weighing 165 pounds. He boasted the most he ever weighed was 180 when he was an enlisted man in the U.S. Army, stationed in The Republic of Korea. Some would consider him handsome. His wife, Princess, was just that. She was part of Sweetwater aristocracy, "Pardon the oxymoron," as Ted would always say as he described her. She was a graduate of McMurray College, now University, Phi Beta Kappa. She had never worked outside the home. She was a graduate of Miss Dorothy's Dance and Voice Studio and had actually gone to New York City to audition for a couple of shows. She had been the darling of Sweetwater her senior year in high school. She loved to sing in the Army chapel choirs, or direct them, and was involved in a local performing arts group in San Antonio.

Ted got out of the Army after his first enlistment to finish his college and then go to seminary. He graduated from Brite Divinity School at Texas Christian University and six months later accessioned to the Army Chaplaincy. He and Princess married after his first year at Brite. He went there to study under Charles F. Kemp, Ph.D., Distinguished Professor of Pastoral Care because he knew he wanted to be an Army Chaplain, not have a career in the local churches of West Texas. While in the Army, he was given the opportunity to do a masters degree in counseling. He was able to parlay that into a Doctor of Psychology degree by taking extra classes and finishing his thesis at his next duty assignment. He then took the Texas State exam and became a licensed psychologist. His terminal assignment was Brooke Army Medical Center, Fort Sam Houston, Texas, two miles from the Central Business District of San Antonio. When he retired in 2001, the position for the Director of PCC had just become available. "Thank you Jeeezus," was his only comment about the timing of that. Princess loved San Antonio because it had such a wonderful society life and it was just the right distance, five hours, from Sweetwater and her overbearing parents.

"The Team" left their 7:30 a.m. meeting at the Cracker Barrel Restaurant, I-10 at Huebner, at the prescribed time to get to the PCS conference room for the weekly nine o'clock staff meeting. Charles had learned the importance of a weekly gathering of leaders from a former boss when he was a chaplain clinician at Harris Methodist Hospital in Ft. Worth. His supervisor liked to have the group share prayer request and then pray in the restaurant. Charles had deleted that segment because he never quite

104

got over the embarrassment of calling attention to the group prayer in a public place. The words of Jesus, or at least what the Gospels said about what he said was, "When you pray, go into your closet to pray...." were quite significant to him and he privately abhorred people who made a big thing out of praying in restaurants, although some of his friends did so.

He had also learned that conflict is best resolved on a full stomach. If anyone had a problem with a colleague, Tuesday morning breakfast was a good place to deal with it. It was rare to have problems among the diverse team, but it did happen, especially when turf was perceived to be threatened.

10/1330 January 2006

"Hello. I'm Ted Anglemeyer," he said as he extended his hand to his new client.

"Hello. Thank you for seeing me. I guess Chaplain Womac told you why I'm here," said Calinda Chavez without making eye contact.

"Please have a seat, anywhere you would like."

"Which one is yours?" asked Calinda, feeling very uneasy and self-conscious. "I don't want to sit in your chair."

"You are welcome to sit wherever you choose. It makes no difference to me." Ted noted to himself that Calinda sat in the chair that looked least comfortable. "Sandy told me you might call. We don't discuss confidential conversations with each other without the person's permission. I'm glad you made an appointment." Ted paused and out waited Calinda's silence.

"Sometimes I think I'm going crazy," she said, hesitantly. Once again there was a heavy silence in the room. "I'm not usually like this." Pause. "I totally lost it after the death of a patient the other day." Silence.

"Help me understand what you mean by 'lost it.' You mean you fell on the ground and started foaming at the mouth?" Ted said with a wry

105

smile.

Calinda looked at him and began smiling as well. "No. I just couldn't stop my tears. Usually, I'm able to control my feelings better than that. I've attended over a hundred deaths. None of them have gotten to me like this one. I didn't even know her. I was off the day she came through the ED. She is, was, a twenty-five year old Hispanic female in a rollover MVA. Her injuries were pretty minor. The worst was a fractured right femur. She wasn't supposed to die. All of us were shocked. It just doesn't make sense."

"Tell me what you think happened," said Ted.

"The autopsy said she threw a PE, uh, pulmonary embolism. The clot went through her heart and into her lung. When I first started nursing, that happened a lot, especially with fractured femurs, but today, it's pretty rare. Just doesn't seem right," said Calinda as she drifted off in thought.

After a couple of moments of silence, Ted said, "I'd like it if you would share some of those thoughts with me."

Calinda blushed slightly and looked embarrassed. "I was thinking about the code. Everyone worked so hard. It wasn't even complicated. Went pretty much the way it should have", pause, "except we didn't get her back. She was gone before we got there. So sad." A tear rolled down her cheek. Then she looked up at Ted as if to say, "Now what?"

"Tell me what kind of feelings you had right after they called the code; sad, happy, lonely, anxious, depressed, angry, worried, scared?"

"I was totally pissed!" said Calinda becoming much more animated. "It was just so wrong. I rushed to the staff restroom before anyone could see me crying. I must have been in there a good five minutes. As I came out, I saw the chaplain going with the doctor to tell the family. Thank God I don't have that job. As I walked down the stairs to the ED, I didn't want to be on the elevator with other people, I started feeling really sad and started thinking about her parents. That's really got to be tough on them. Later I heard the father has a heart condition. I cried a little more and when I got to the first floor, I leaned against the wall in the stairwell until I could get it together."

"Tell me what your role was in the resuscitation attempt," said Ted, softly.

Calinda described, in some detail, how the team effort went and what she had done. After a few minutes of clinical description, she said, "I've been over it a hundred times and I can't find anything that any of us did wrong. It was just how they taught us to do it. We're really good at what we do. It just wasn't enough."

"Tell me what it's been like for you since then."

"Pretty bumpy. I've had problems sleeping. A lot of crazy dreams when I do. I've also had a lot of weird thoughts."

"Intrusive thoughts," suggested Ted.

"Yeah. Especially when I'm driving home or when we have a code blue somewhere in the hospital. The other day, I almost ran a red light on Fredericksburg at Medical Drive. I was just off somewhere thinking about the code."

"Any changes in eating habits and/or fatigue levels?"

"Yeah, the first couple of days I had no appetite at all and now I stand at the refrigerator and if it's not moving, I eat it. My clothes are starting to get a little tight," said Calinda pulling at the top to her scrubs. "I'm also really tired a lot. I just can't seem to get my energy back."

"Any loss of enjoyment in things you used to like doing?" asked Ted.

"A lot. I haven't kept up with my TV shows and," pause, "And sex is totally out of the question." She looked at the Reverend Doctor Ted Anglemeyer to see how he would react.

"That's not normal for you."

"Not at all. I love my husband and we have a pretty good sex life, but lately I just haven't been in the mood. Ramón is starting to get irritated about that." She thought for a few seconds and then said, "And I have been cursing a lot lately. That's not like me. I'm a good Catholic girl, you know?" she said with a brief twinkle in her eye and a smile.

"So you're pretty angry, still."

"Yeah, I guess I am. It just doesn't seem fair."

"No it's not," said Ted. "It's not fair at all. Tell me what other feelings you've been having."

"Father, why does God let things like this happen? Oh, I'm sorry, I meant Chaplain. Is that what I'm supposed to call you? Or should I say, Doctor?"

"'Ted' works best for me, but you can call me whatever you are most comfortable with. I'm always complimented when someone calls me Father. I know it's a term of real respect for Catholics and Episcopalians." Pause. "So, sounds like you're angry with God."

"Yeah, I guess I am. I know the sisters use to tell us we're not supposed to be angry with God, but sometimes I am. Why did he let her die? That's not fair. He could have saved her. He could have told the doctors what to do. Sometimes I just wonder what the hell God is thinking."

"It just doesn't make sense," Ted reflected. Calinda shook her head as she began crying, again. Pause. "Seems to me, if anyone can handle our anger, it's God. I mean, I get angry at God rather frequently. Especially when I see or hear of things like what you're describing. I've even told God off a few times and at least so far I haven't seen any lightning bolts sent my way. Sometimes it really helps to shake your fist in the face of God and get that hurt and fear out."

"You mean it's okay to be angry with Him?"

"If anyone understands, it's God." Pause. "Far be it for me to contradict a Roman Catholic nun, but so far, God and I have gotten along okay with me getting angry occasionally. As a parent, I'd much rather have one of my kids call me every name in the book than to just walk away and never have anything to do with me, again. That would break my heart."

"I guess I see what you mean. I wouldn't want *mis hijos* to do that to me. I love them too much for that. My kids are my heart."

"Tell me what other feelings you've been having."

"I'm not sure. What was that list, again?"

"Sad, happy, lonely, anxious, depressed, angry, worried, scared," Ted reiterated.

"Well, I certainly haven't been very happy, lately. I guess pretty worried,…"

"About?"

"About whether or not I'm going crazy."

"Sometimes you feel like you're going crazy," added Ted.

"Yeah, I do. All these uninvited thoughts and not sleeping and feeling hopeless sometimes. Like nothing we do really makes a difference. People still die and families grieve. I feel so helpless." Ted sat quietly as she allowed herself to feel the pain. "It just seems so futile sometimes."

"Tell me, what was the worst part, for you?"

Without hesitating, Calinda blurted, "When Dr. Washington told Dr. Sassmann to call it. I just wanted to scream at them to keep going, but I realized it was futile at the same time. I didn't know what I wanted."

"Sounds like you wanted to save her, to keep her from dying," said Ted with a comforting tone.

Calinda began to sob.

After a moment, Ted said, "That's good, let it go Calinda. Just let it all go."

The crying continued for at least four minutes. The sobs would slow and then a new rush would come. Ted sat in silence giving her the space and permission she needed to express such deep pain. Then a sound like a wounded animal came from deep inside her. Ted moved to her chair and asked if he could touch her back. She nodded and he gently placed his hand between her shoulder blades, above her bra strap, and slowly moved it up to the base of her neck. He did so a number of times as this triggered more of the agony Calinda had carried for so long. As she began to calm and the sobbing ended, he stepped away and sat in his chair, waiting. Shortly, Calinda reached for the tissues on the coffee table and began to wipe her eyes and face. Then she blew her nose, and leaned back against her chair. In a moment, she looked directly at Ted. He smiled and said, "You really did some hard work, there. Thank you for your compliment of trusting me to do that."

"I guess I felt safe. I haven't cried like that in a very long time." Calinda took a deep breath and audibly exhaled.

"Tell me where you see hope in all this."

"Hmm. I guess I still know how to do my job and we have had a couple of successful resuscitations in the trauma room since the one we've been talking about. It's funny, but *I* don't even know the patient's name that died last Tuesday. I just know it hurt like hell."

"Aren't you glad it did?" He paused for a full two minutes as she processed his comment. "If you can go through something like that and not feel at least some pain, you're well past burnout and we've all seen that in our colleagues. It ain't pretty."

"Amen, to that." Pause. "Thank you. I feel much better."

"I'd like to respond to what I see happening. It's sort of like a good news/bad news joke. I'm not trying to be flippant. You'll see what I mean in just a minute. Based on everything you have told me, it's my professional opinion that you are one hundred percent normal. That's the good news. The bad news is you are one hundred percent normal, and that hurts really badly."

"I'm not *loco*?"

"Not even close. Your reaction to an abnormal situation is totally normal," said Ted reassuringly. "What has happened is that you have been traumatized by this event. That's why I took you through what we call an informal debriefing of the event. It helps mitigate the impact. Also, I'd like for you to take one of these pamphlets on Post Traumatic Stress. You might see some things that look familiar. It also has a list of things on the back you can do for yourself to get through this. Hopefully, it will help."

"But we see people die all the time. Why did this one hit me so hard?"

"I'm not sure. That may be something we could look at, another time."

Calinda thought for a moment. "You know, when I was talking to Chaplain Womac, she asked when the first time I had a reaction like this was. Do you think there's a connection?"

"Very well could be. Why don't we work on that next time? I have another client in a few minutes. Just talk to my assistant out front and she

110

can schedule an appointment for next week. Does this seem like a place to stop, for today?"

"Yes. Thank you, uh, Ted. I really appreciate your help."

"You're very welcome. See you next week," said Ted as he walked her to the door of his office. Upon closing it, he thought to himself, *sure glad I'm not Ramón. I'm too damned old to take a roll in the hay like he's going to get tonight.*

10/2200 January 2006

Chaplain (Resident) Jaime Martinez, M. Div., felt the vibration of his pager against his right side where it hung on his belt. He deftly removed it and began to read the scrolling text: "Duty chaplain to MICU, stat." His pace quickened as he headed for the elevator. After an interminable period, he arrived at the seventh floor, walked off the elevator and headed straight for the nurses' station in the Medical Intensive Care Unit. When the unit secretary looked up and saw Jaime, a look of relief replaced the expression of total frustration.

"How may I be useful to you, today, Ms. Walton?" said Jaime who was trying to look more confident than he was.

"The nurses wanted the duty chaplain here because we have a young woman whom they brought in this morning with an unknown infection. She's probably not going to make it and the husband is very angry. They are afraid he might cause trouble."

"I'll see what I can do. Was Chaplain Pena with him today?" asked Jaime.

"I don't know. I didn't come on until three and I haven't seen him. Of course, she wasn't put on the critical list until 1630. He probably missed it."

"Where's the husband?"

"He's been in the waiting room. The doctors have been working on

111

her non-stop since I got here."

"What's the patient's name?" asked Jaime.

"Haley Simons. Twenty-seven year old Caucasian female, unknown infection which is not responding to antibiotics."

"Do you know the last time anyone gave him an update or when he saw his wife?"

"One of the nurses went out about fifteen minutes ago to talk with him. That's when they decided to call you. He hasn't been in to see her since I got here. That's about all I know, Chaplain. You might want to talk to the doctor or a nurse before you go out to see him."

"Good idea, Ms. Walton. Thank you. I need all the help I can get."

"I think you're going to need it, Chaplain. This one could be real tough."

I feel better, already. Not! With encouragement like that, who needs whatever the heck it is I need? Whatever it is, I ain't got it. Jaime walked to the glass cubicle where all the action was. Several staff were wearing universal precautions including masks, booties, and hair nets. A large sign hastily taped to the wall said: ISOLATION, UNIVERSAL PRECAUTIONS REQUIRED AT ALL TIMES. *Guess that's clear enough* thought Jaime as he picked up a mask, held it over his nose and wrapped on the glass. When one of the doctors turned to see what the noise was, Jaime told her he was going to see the husband and asked if she had anything she wanted him to tell Mr. Simons.

"Tell him she's really sick and we're doing everything we can," said the doctor with great frustration in her voice. "I'll try to get out to see him when things slow down."

Jaime turned to walk away as he heard one of the nurses say, "If you know any good prayers, Padre, now's the time to say them."

"Got it," he said as he stood in the doorway facing the staff and made the sign of the cross over them. He picked up his pace as he walked down the corridor.

"Mr. Simons? I'm Chaplain Jaime Martinez. The doctor asked me to come by and say hello."

"Go back in there and talk to my wife. She's the one who needs you, not me," he said very angrily. "I don't need anyone saying prayers over me."

"This must be very frightening. I understand your wife just came to the hospital this morning. Has she been feeling ill, lately?"

"Hell no. She was feeling great this morning. We went shopping to get some things for the new apartment. We've just been in San Antonio a couple of weeks. I got a job offer and we came down from Michigan. This is the first day off I've had in ten days. We went shopping and around ten a. m., she started feeling bad and by eleven said she thought we should go to the hospital. They saw her in the E.R. and then rushed her up here. They don't even know what's wrong with her. They just said she has an infection."

"When was the last time someone gave you an update on how she's doing?" asked Jaime.

The husband looked at Jaime as if he had just said the moon was made of green cheese. "How the hell should I know? No one has said jack shit to me since before it got dark." *That would be about 5:30. What about the nurse who said she talked to him fifteen minutes ago? This is not going well.* The husband had the look of a caged animal. After a moment, he stared at Jaime and said, "Why the hell did they call you? Is she going to die, or something? Are you here because they've given up on her?" His voice was rising with every question, as was his panic.

"They called me because the rest of the staff is so busy trying to help your wife. They wanted someone to be here for you. No one has given up. Before I came out here to meet you, the doctor told me that they are doing everything they can."

113

"How is she doing? Is my wife getting any better?"

"The doctor told me to tell you she is critically ill and that they are very concerned for her. They asked that I sit with you for a while. Is that okay?" The man just nodded slowly as he stared at the floor. "Thank you. I'm not here to invade your privacy. I just wanted to keep you company until we hear something from the doctor. I'll leave anytime you tell me you want me to go." *"That's good, Jaime, give them lots of choices so they will have at least some control,"* the fledgling clinician heard Sister Joyce say. The man made no response. *Wait for it. Wait for it.* When he couldn't stand the silence any longer he said, "So you've only been here two weeks? Do you have any family in the area?" The man shook his head. "Must be pretty lonely. Have you made any friends?"

"I have met some guys at work. It's been pretty hard on Haley. She comes from a big family and really misses them. Plus we grew up in the same small town where everyone knows everyone. There just wasn't any work up there. We've been married for four years and this is the first time I've had a job that wasn't minimum wage. We thought we'd found the Promised Land…and now this."

"What line of work are you in?" asked Jaime. *Shit, should have used active listening. You blew it again, genius.*

"I'm a welder. I got on with AAA Salvage down here. The pay's real good and we like San Antonio. Or at least what little we've seen of it. We want to start a family as soon as we get settled."

"Sounds like you have some big plans."

"Yeah, or at least we did." The man's bitterness was palpable.

Jaime's pager began to vibrate and he knew it wasn't someone texting to say "Have a great day." *It never is.* PLEASE REPORT TO THE NURSES' STATION, MICU. After reading the message he looked at the forlorn man and said, "I'm going to go check on Haley. I'll be back in just a few minutes." The man began to stare at the floor, again.

No one needed to tell the chaplain resident what had happened. The patient was dead. One or two of the nurses had moist eyes and the physician had tears on her cheeks and in her eyes. She pulled off her mask as she walked out of the cubicle, and he recognized her as Dr. Patricia Flores, an Internal Medicine Resident III. They had "worked" a couple of other cases together and Jaime enjoyed her presence.

She was very caring and competent and she was a homey from South San Antonio, Highlands High School to be exact and she had made good. Undergrad at Rice University and then med school at University of Texas Medical School in Galveston, Texas. She was a very pretty *Hispana*, in Jaime's opinion, five foot three with dark brown eyes that could melt a heart of stone. They had never spent any "one on one" time together but Jaime liked the way she did business in these kinds of situations. He was feeling a little relieved.

"Thanks for being here, Chaplain. This is really a tough one. Will you go with me to tell the husband?" asked the doctor.

"Yes, of course. I just need to get security up here before we go out there." He turned away from the shocked resident and walked to the nurses' station. Without waiting for Ms. Walton to acknowledge him, he said, "I need you to get security up here stat. I want them to stay out of sight of the waiting room, but I want them here, just in case."

"Are you sure?" the unit secretary asked.

"Very. That guy is mad as a wet hen and being told his wife is dead is not going to improve his mood. It's not in my job description to take punches from an irate family member." Ms. Walton immediately did as she was asked, adding her instructions to the person on the other end of the phone line to notify her as soon as the officer was in place. Jaime used his time to let Dr. Flores vent some of her frustration over never being able to get ahead of the infection and her patient's quick demise.

The unit phone rang. "MICU, Ms. Walton." She listened for a moment and then said, "Thank you very much for your quick response. Good-bye." She looked at Jaime and simply said, "Security is in place."

"Guess it's show time," Jaime said to Patricia. "How do you want to play it?"

"Whatever you think best, Chaplain."

Chicanas are so much easier to work with. They recognize the authority of

115

the male, thought Jaime, facetiously. *Think I'll just keep that appreciation of the culture to myself. Don't want to push my luck.* "Have you met Mr. Simons?"

The doctor shook her head. "The hospitalist, Doctor Solonese, talked to him earlier. I was busy in here for the last several hours. Damned waste of time. She never had a chance. I can't imagine what bug she was growing. It was some seriously bad mokus."

"I'll introduce you to Mr. Simons. Then we'll sit and I'll let you do the notification. Take as long as you want. He's not ready for this and he may become violent. That's why I asked for security. I don't think he'll go off on you or me, but for a *Gringo,* he sure acts like an *Hispano.* Hit something first and then go off."

"Yeah, I've seen that a time or two, before. *Pendejos chingada.*"

Jaime was taken off guard by Patricia's profanity. He recovered quickly, "Feel free to stand behind me until security gets here if he goes off," said Jaime with a wink and a grin.

They walked out of the MICU and immediately saw the security officer standing against the wall at the end of the short corridor. When they reached him, Jaime extended his hand and said, "I'm Chaplain Martinez and this is Dr. Flores. I hope we don't need you, but better to have you here in case we do. Just stay out of sight unless you hear something being broken. With any luck, the man we are about to tell his wife just died will not have to see you—nothing personal." The officer just nodded and leaned back against the wall. Jaime took a deep breath and let it out slowly, saying a short prayer in his head for guidance. "Ready?" he said to a very frightened young doctor. She nodded and Jaime led the way.

"Mr. Simons." The chaplain resident said. Immediately the man's head shot up to look at Jaime and the white coated woman standing before him. "This is Doctor Flores. She has been taking care of your wife this evening." The man slowly began to comprehend this was not going to end well.

An eternity later, they were all seated and Dr. Flores leaned toward the ashen man. "Mr. Simons, when Haley got to the unit this morning, Dr. Solonese and I assessed that she had a pervasive infection of an unknown

116

origin and type. We still don't know what it is, because it takes twenty-four to thirty-six hours to grow a culture." Patricia waited until she saw some comprehension in the man's face. "We immediately put her on the strongest antibiotics we have and treated her for a number of abnormal vital functions." The man looked confused. "We had to give her medicine to regulate her heart rate, blood pressure, urine output, and eventually her breathing. We also had to work to keep her temperature within an acceptable range." She paused again. The man nodded as if to say "Tell me more." "Mr. Simons, we did everything we possibly could." Pause. "We were unsuccessful in saving your wife. I'm terribly sorry."

"You mean she's dead?" he said in a quiet tone that shocked both the doctor and the chaplain.

"Yes," said the doctor, her eyes becoming moist.

The man simply lowered his head and cried very softly. Jaime put his hand on his shoulder. When he stopped, Jaime said, "I'm very sorry. I know this has to hurt really badly." When there was no response, he asked, "Do you have any questions for the Doctor?"

The man thought for a moment, shook his head in disbelief and then asked, "May I see her?"

"Yes, the nurses are getting her ready, now. Chaplain will take you in to be with her in a few minutes. Is there anything I can do for you, right now?

"Not unless you know how to bring her back."

"I truly wish I did. I'm very sorry for your loss. We did everything there was to do. I wish there had been more. If you think of anything later, you can reach me through the hospital operator. I'm very sorry." Patricia gently touched his other shoulder as she stood to leave. "Chaplain, I have to get back to the unit. Would you explain to Mr. Simons about the post?"

"Of course. I'll see you, shortly." The Resident III left the chaplain and the widower sitting in silence. She began to think about what she had to do next and of the patients she had neglected for the last few hours.

"What's a post?"

"That's short for post mortem examination." The man still looked confused. "It's an autopsy." Jaime then explained Texas state law concerning patients dying in less than twenty-four hours after admission. "It should be able to tell you what the infection was and why it was so aggressive."

"How long before I can ship her home? Her family will want to see her as soon as possible."

"I understand. I'm not completely sure. You will need to come back to the hospital tomorrow during business hours to talk to someone in the decedent affairs office to begin making arrangements. They will be very helpful." The quote from Sr. Joyce shot through his head. *Don't make promises someone else has to keep.* "At least that's been my experience. I'm assuming you don't have a funeral home in mind. I know this is horribly sudden. The post will **probably** take place tomorrow morning. That means the body can be released as early as tomorrow afternoon. My experience is that there are some laws concerning interstate shipment of a body and the funeral home here will have to do some initial preparation before your funeral home in Michigan can prepare her for the funeral. At least I think that's how it works." Jaime noticed that the man was strictly business and not emoting at all. *Denial and avoidance. The two main coping mechanisms of American males,* thought the young chaplain. This time, it was a quote from Dr. Charles D. McRae, VP for Pastoral Care Services, MHS.

"Are you about ready to go see Haley?"

"Sure, if that's the next box we have to check."

"You don't have to, but I would encourage it. It will help you in the long run. I'm going to go see if the nurses are finished. I'll be right back." He walked away, not waiting for a response. When he rounded the corner, he saw the security guard still in place. *Chingada. I completely forgot about him.* "Hey. Thanks for being here. Everything went fine. I really appreciate your help."

"I didn't do anything," said the young guard.

"Yeah you did. Your presence kept me and the good doctor from freaking. Very important! Thanks, again. See you around the campus."

"Sure. See you later, Chaplain."

I wonder if that's anything like that "Ministry of Presence" Sister is always talking about? Guess I'll have to ask her. Amazing how much better I felt just knowing he was here. I really didn't see Mr. Simons' reaction coming. I figured he'd be throwing chairs, cursing and threatening to kick my ass when Patricia laid the bad news on him. You just never know. "Be ready for anything" is precisely the right approach. Glad I paid attention when Dr. Conyers did that didactic on death notification. Guess he does know what he's doing, after all.

10/2330 January 2006

Jaime had taken the young widower to see the body of his wife. Everything was within normal limits. All that was left was to walk him to the door of the ED and then "go catch butterflies" with the staff. *Easy peezy. Not!* Surprisingly, Jaime was having trouble maintaining his "professional distance." He was hurting for this man whose whole life had just been turned upside down and then sideways. "Is there anyone you would like to call? A neighbor or friend?"

"No thanks. I just need to go home, I mean back to the apartment, and call family. That's going to take a while."

"Another chaplain will be around tomorrow afternoon if you would like to talk. Here's my card. I hope everything goes as well for you as it possibly can. You will be in my prayers." The words seemed to turn to sawdust in Jaime's mouth as he said them. They sounded so hollow—to him. He couldn't imagine how meaningless they sounded to the man who had just lost his wife. The man walked toward the parking lot with a hospital issued plastic bag containing the now useless possessions of his dead wife. His shoulders drooped and his head was down. Jaime wanted to run after him to console him. Or at least make himself feel less useless. He turned and walked back into the bustling ED. The clock on the wall above the nurses' desk said twenty-three thirty-seven. *Crap! I still need to go check*

119

on the staff. Maybe Patricia will be around. It would be nice to have a cup of coffee with her. Hello! Trauma bonding! Jaime headed straight to the day room next to the office of the Director for Clinical Chaplaincy Services to log in the death. *I'll go check on the staff in a few minutes. Maybe Patricia will be gone by then. Hopefully by then I can get my testosterone under control.*

CHAPTER 9

12/1600 January 2006

"Damn it, Chuck, you can't do that!" exclaimed Trevor Conyers, D. Min., LPC, LMFT, BCC, Director of Clinical Chaplaincy Services.

Charles McRae waited a moment before responding. As calmly and quietly as possible he looked at the Director and said, "We don't really have much choice. Victoria stepped over the line and the entire Service will be discredited if we don't play by the same rules as everyone else. I know she meant no harm, but she made a really dumb mistake and we can't unring the bell."

"Victoria Stone is one of the best PRN chaplains we have. I can't remember the last time she said 'no' when I asked her to pull a shift. She's always available when we need her. Do you realize what that's worth in and of itself? And she's a damned good SAFE chaplain as well. I don't need to tell you we're running short in that department."

"No you don't. I agree with everything you say about her. I don't want to fire her. She's a good kid with some real potential, but this just can't be swept under the rug. I'm directing you to terminate her employment, immediately." Charles paused to let that sink in.

"Yes sir."

"Do you want me to sit in when you tell her?"

"No sir. I'm a big boy and this is why I make the big bucks. I know we're doing the correct thing, but we're not doing the right thing."

"I understand. One of the reasons I hired you for this position is that you have a pastor's heart. Our people take beatings every day, of one kind or another. I rely on you to shepherd them and provide the care they need to keep going. Even when you have to do something like this, you do it in love. I wish there was another option."

"Yes sir. I'll let you know when the deed is done. Is there anything else, sir?"

"No." Charles caught himself before he said "That will be all." *I don't want to get into this military mentality too much. It does help though that he has that back ground. He's a good troop even when he doesn't want to be.*

Yesterday, the Vice President for Human Resources had given Charles a courtesy call to tell him a sexual harassment complaint had been filed against one of his chaplains, Victoria Stone, M. Div. He immediately informed Trevor, who then called in Victoria to hear her side of the story. She admitted that she had been handling a Sexual Assault Forensic Evidence case at Methodist Specialty Hospital, just three blocks from 'Big Methodist', when she and the mother of a rape survivor were waiting with a friend while the forensic evidence nurse and advocate from the Rape Crisis Services Center were doing the "rape kit" on her daughter in the next room.

All reports indicated that they were actually talking and joking about the fact all three of them had large breasts and were relating humorous stories about it. It was 0300 and they were all running on nervous energy and adrenalin. As they began to laugh rather hysterically, Victoria poked the mom's breast as an act of misguided frivolity. The woman never said anything and upon later investigation had no problem with what had happened. But the friend in the room did. She filed the complaint.

It was a very clear, *and very stupid* thought Charles, violation of the System's Sexual Ethics Policy. It was also a clear violation of the SWTC Sexual Ethics Policy. Even though Victoria was not United Methodist, that is the policy all chaplains are expected to follow in addition to the one of MMHS. The SWTC policy was more extensive and specific for clergy than the other. Those expectations had been communicated to all chap-

122

lains in MMHS verbally as well as in writing at least annually.

Charles hated giving directives as specific as the one he gave Trevor. He really hated firing someone as competent, in all other areas, as Victoria. He had hoped to hire her full time when he had a position that required her skill set. She would make a great pediatric chaplain—especially to fill John Allison's slot if he went to the new hospital. *The best laid plans…usually get screwed up by human stupidity. Shit.*

The intercom on his desk buzzed. When he picked up the receiver, Anna, his administrative assistant/PCS Office Manager said, "Your five o'clock is here. Anything you need from me before I leave for the day?"

"Nothing I can think of at the moment. Have a good evening. Please tell her I'll be out there in a minute. I need to decompress before I start a counseling session."

"You got it, chief." She loved calling him that because Trevor Conyers always put "Chief's Time" on the agenda of the quarterly Service meetings. She assumed it had something to do with his military background. Trevor ran the meetings because he was the Pastoral Care Services deputy director. That too was a military thing that he had convinced Charles he should do rather than run the meetings himself. The first time she saw an agenda, she immediately thought, with a chuckle, they would play "Hail to the Chief" when it was Charles' turn to speak. She had told him that story later and it was a private joke between them.

Charles had great respect and affection for Anna. She was sixth generation San Antonian. Her forbearer had been a civilian black smith with Santa Anna's army at the battle of the Alamo, 23 February--6 March 1836. The family story was he liked the *pueblo* (small town) of what was to become the nation's seventh largest city and opted to stay there rather than continue on with the Mexican army and its defeat at the battle of *San Jacinto*, 21 April 1836. The Gutierrez family had been in San Antonio since. Anna had worked for Methodist Hospital since graduating from Jefferson High School in 1970. She later got her Associates degree in Secretarial Skills from San Antonio Community College, while working full time at MMHS.

Anna was always pleasant and efficient as well as being the institutional memory for the Service and the hospital. One year after MMHS was created, Anna applied and was hired for the secretary position of the Department of Education and Training, PCS. When the System went through its first major budget reductions, every major Department had to reduce staff Full Time Equivalencies by ten percent. Charles and his team of Directors elected to eliminate the position for his administrative assistant. Sister wasn't crazy about having to share Anna's time with Charles, but she understood and accepted the decision. They also eliminated two FTEs of clinicians. Anna had risen to the occasion and proved herself worthy of Charles' trust. He learned to rely on her for her opinion and insight into many of the complex issues about which he had to make decisions.

Charles made good on his promise to Joyce as soon as finances allowed. He promoted Anna to Office Manager for Pastoral Care Services, which gave her a raise in pay as well as status among the administrative support personnel of the System. He then hired someone for the position she vacated, Sarah. Not all personnel decisions work as well as one anticipates. Sarah quit after fourteen months to care for her ailing father and it was a win-win for all. Anna had grown professionally by that time to assert herself more in the selection process and they were able to hire a competent person, Bianca Mendes, who was a grand addition to the team. Sister Joyce was pleased, which in turn pleased Charles.

12/1705 January 2006

"Hello, Theresa. Welcome and come on back," said Charles as he smiled at his client of six months.

"¡*Hola*!, Doctor McRae," replied the svelte, beautiful, forty-two year old blond. She was wearing a slinky dress that was cut too low for that time of day. "I've been looking forward to seeing you all week. I have soooo much to tell you. I just can't wait." *Oh, neither can I dear Theresa, neither can I*, thought Charles, as his internal sarcasm went into hyper drive. He led the way to his office at the back of the suite. *I am so glad I set it up for Ted to check the reverse peep hole in the door.* His office was just across the hall and they frequently checked on the other to verify nothing inappropriate was happening during a session. The Reverend Doctor Ted Anglemeyer had recommended they do that soon after the Pastoral Counseling Center was founded. He had learned the trick from a fellow Army Chaplain with whom he had served in Nuremberg. This also applied to Ted and the PCC office. The peep holes, like those in front doors across the nation, were installed such that someone in the hallway outside the closed door of an office being used for counseling could get the "fish eye" view of the entire interior space. Everyone was trained to check the goings on in the office when they passed, to ensure false allegations of misconduct could be negated. Law suits and/or allegations have a way of damaging careers and reputations.

Theresa Birdsong was "hot" by any straight man's estimation. She also suffered from a condition that one psychiatrist had identified in a client many years before, during a group clinical supervisory session. Following a formal case presentation to the "group soup" in which the aspiring young psychotherapist had busted his butt to prepare, the Shrink just said, "Chuck, I think she's just crazier than dog shit." That became a lasting diagnosis for Charles through his years as a Licensed Professional Counselor. In keeping with the tradition of the Diagnostic and Statistical Manual-IV-TR and its predecessors, he had reduced the diagnosis to CTDS. It was occasionally used among the staff of the Pastoral Care Center as well as the Leadership Team of PCS. Theresa's picture would have been in the DSM-IV-TR had it been listed as an actual personality disorder.

She had a real dual diagnosis of Borderline Personality Disorder and Bipolar Disorder. In her case, it was manifest in extremely poor decisions, especially about attire and having extra marital sexual encounters. This was complicated by the fact her husband was a well respected physician and subspecialist at MMHS. He had sought Charles' help when the latest affair, with an auto mechanic, had occurred. Charles frequently did therapy with physicians and senior administrators. He considered himself their workplace pastor and made a point of randomly appearing in their work places.

The first time he donned scrubs, mask, shower cap, booties and sterile gloves and walked into an operating room, he established himself as not your normal, garden variety Father Mulcahy. He wanted people, surgeons particularly, to know that he was there for them and the OR staff. Nurses loved it. With the docs, he got mixed reviews. But then, only the Church is slower to adjust to change than some physicians. A few of them thought he had been sent there to be a spy for Administration. Charles put appropriate information into the right ears, e.g., Bill Groene, the Chief of Staff and a few well known surgeons, Taylor Birdsong, MD for one, and the problem went away, quietly.

"Please have a seat, Theresa. Would you like a cup of tea?"

"No, thank you."

"So tell me how you have been."

"This last week has been so crazy. Donny and I went on a four day trip to Vegas and it was so wonderful!" Theresa said. She elaborated in vivid detail the events of the trip. When she started to talk about the best sex she had ever had, Charles interrupted.

"Theresa, as I have shared with you before, it's not necessary or even preferable to go into those kinds of details. I think the more relevant issue is your choosing to act out your anger toward Taylor and your father with unprotected, high risk sex. What's that about?" Charles was aware that he was being uncharacteristically confrontive. The first two sessions with Theresa were a cacophony of detailed descriptions of her latest sexual exploits. He recognized the "test" she was administering to see if he, as clergy, would react to her language and history. She was disappointed when he did not. He also identified her Borderline Personality Disorder halfway through the first session. *"Boundaries, boundaries, boundaries"* he heard his former psychiatric consultant say, in his head.

"I don't know," she said with a wicked smile.

126

"I think you do. We've talked about this before."

"Well, my brilliant therapist says it's my way of getting back at my daddy for incesting me and men in general for never living up to my unrealistically high expectations."

"I said all that? I don't remember that diatribe," said Charles.

"Well you did in so many words." Pause. "Over several sessions I guess." More silence. "At least that's what I took from it. Or maybe it was what you said and that book you made me read, I Hate You, Don't Leave Me."

"The book I **made** you read? Gee, I didn't realize I was so powerful," he said with a slight smile.

"Okay, the book I **chose** to read—based on your recommendation. I **always** do what you suggest, **Doctor** McRae."

"If that's true, why were you in Las Vegas, this last weekend? I feel pretty confident, had you asked, I would have recommended against it."

"That's why I didn't ask. I just wanted to have some fun. Taylor will never know, so what difference does it make?" she asked with feigned innocence.

"If you were me, what would you tell you?"

"I guess you would say that self-destructive behavior leads to negative consequences and that it hurts my marriage."

"And what would you say?" asked Charles.

The conversation went on like that for another thirty minutes. Charles was really growing tired of the banter and Theresa's unwillingness, or inability to set even the simplest of boundaries. Finally, the time set aside for the session was exhausted and so was he.

"Does this seem like a place we might quit for today? Our time is up."

"Oh. I was getting to the best part…"

"Let's save the best part for next week. It's not a good idea to start a new topic, now. Same time, next week?" asked Charles.

Theresa sighed, bent over at the waist to pick her purse off the floor, and immodestly revealed her lovely set of augmented breasts. Charles

127

worked hard to not roll his eyes or stare. Instead, he just stood and walked to the door to open it for his client as she exited with her usual flourish.

"Good-bye, Doctor," Theresa said oozing charm and seduction. *Thank God that's over. Our sessions absolutely wear me out. Maybe I could refer her? Come on, McRae, grow a pair and don't even think about using them.*

The majority of time, Charles enjoyed doing therapy. He loved watching people grow through their pain. "It's like watching one of those old Disney time-lapse photography clips of a flower opening," he had said a number of times. He had worked with people who had been through horrible, ongoing abuse and trauma. These were people of whom he said if they could get up, get their clothes on and get to work they had had a successful day. Everything else was gravy. He had seen people grow through unbelievable pain and yet have a positive attitude toward life that the privileged only wished for.

He encouraged all of his chaplains who were licensed to do therapy as the opportunities presented themselves. If they saw a staff member or one of the staff's family members, it counted as Employee Assistance Program hours. If they were PCC clients, they were charged on a sliding scale based on income and family members, or their insurance was billed through the business office. EAP cases counted as "cost avoidance" and the "hard dollars" were clearly revenue. The symbolic significance was much more important than the actual money. It showed that Pastoral Care Services was a revenue center, not just overhead. Theresa Birdsong was a "Full pay" at the rate of $100/hour. *I'm still not sure it's worth it, at least days like today.*

13/2234 January 2006

Chaplain (Resident) Sandy Womac, M. Div., had just finished handling another death with "Dr. Assmann." Once again, there had been some tension between them, particularly when he had cut her off in midsentence while she was trying to explain about the family needing to report to decedent affairs the next day. "If you have any questions of me later, you can call the hospital operator to speak with me. I'm sorry for your loss." With that he turned on his heel and was gone.

Sandy flushed with anger, took a deep breath and then continued talking with the family in as pastoral a way as possible under the circumstances. She prepped the family to see their loved one's body, took them in to see him, and then walked them to the front door of the hospital. It had become rote for her. She hoped the family had not picked up on that. She was still processing her anger with "Dr. Assman," as she had come to think of him, at least when she wasn't having intrusive thoughts of him half naked as he was gently touching her arm, shoulder, neck or face. Once he was touching her breast in a totally pleasing way for her, until she literally shook her head to get the thought out of her consciousness. She could never completely determine if the thoughts were pleasing or disturbing.

"Maybe they're both," said Sister Joyce when Sandy had reluctantly shared them in her private supervision session last week. Sandy was completely confused at that point. She just couldn't make sense of the unwanted thoughts.

"What do you think they mean, Sister?" asked Sandy.

"I don't know," said her supervisor with an all-knowing smile. "What do you think they mean, Sandy?"

"I wish I knew. I mean, he is nice looking and he can be quite kind with patients and families, but he's just such an ass where I'm concerned. He seems to go out of his way to cut me off when I'm speaking, or be arrogant in front of his peers when I'm present." Pause.

"Hmmm," mused Sister Joyce. "Well, our time is up for today. I'll see you at didactics in the morning." The good Sister's smile was a little less blatant as Sandy left her office.

13/2347 January 2006

"Chaplain, may I have a word with you?" asked Karl T. Sassmann, MD. His tone made it more a dictate than an invitation. Sandy sighed heavily, expecting a confrontation. She almost welcomed it so she could tell him what an insensitive jerk he was. She was fed up with the way he had been treating her. She was pleased when he led her to an empty exam room and closed the door. She didn't want the staff to hear what she had to say to him. When he turned from the door, he took one step, enfolded her in his arms and kissed her, gently at first and then with passion.

Sandy's entire body tensed as her eyes widened to their maximum. Then she felt herself melt in Karl's arms and began to respond with equal pressure of her lips to his. It may have been a second or five minutes before his embrace began to relax. She had no way of knowing. When he pulled his face from hers, he looked deeply into her eyes.

"I've wanted to do that since the first time I saw you. It just took a while to work up the courage. I'd really like to take you to breakfast when we go off shift in the morning." She hesitated, imperceptibly, and then stood on her tip toes to kiss him. This time it was more passion and less tenderness. They played smacky face for a few minutes until their pagers buzzed simultaneously. "TRAUMA TEAM TO THE TRAUMA ROOM. MULTIPLE GSWs FIVE MINUTES OUT."

"Now what do we do?" asked a confused, frightened, frustrated and exhilarated Sandy.

"Go to the trauma room?" he asked. She looked at him questioningly. "I'll go first, you count to one hundred by fives and then come out." With no further hesitation he was gone.

A weak kneed Chaplain (Resident) Womac began to count, "Five, ten, fifteen...*What the fuck are you doing, Sandra? This isn't a goddamned game of hide and go seek.*" She ran her fingers through her hair, adjusted her scrubs, tried to smooth out a couple of wrinkles in them and checked her lipstick in the mirror to ensure it wasn't smeared.

"Its show time," she said to herself as she walked out the door. Once she was in the hall, she focused completely on the door to the trauma room. She could see the flashing lights of the arriving ambulance. *It's never five minutes*, she thought as she began to put on the ugly yellow plastic protective over-blouse. She put on her protective goggles/glasses and grabbed a pair of exam gloves, size small, and then walked toward the patient as the EMTs began to exit with their gurney.

Sandy had heard enough of their report to Dr. Sassmann and staff to know this was the most serious of the three gunshot wound patients they would be receiving in rapid succession. He was a twenty-one year old Hispanic male with all the tatts of a gang banger. She stepped to his left shoulder and began her *spiel* as the staff started cutting off his clothes. She smelled alcohol on his breath as she leaned close to his ear and said, "Hi, I'm Chaplain Womac-and-they-call-me-for-all-of-these. What's your name?" The young man looked at her with disapproval and confusion.

"You ain't no fucking priest. You think I'm stupid or something?" The patient said with no little contempt in his voice.

"No, I'm not a fucking priest. I'm an ordained Presbyterian minister and a hospital chaplain. And yes, I think you're stupid. You're obviously a gang banger and you forgot to duck." A couple of the nurses had great difficulty not laughing. Dr. Sassmann winked at her with his left eye, the one the staff couldn't see. She asked the patient what happened.

"Me and some of my homeys was just hanging out on our corner and this low rider came by packed with "Bloods." They started firing before we knew what was happening. Nacho got hit first, then me."

"Tell me what happened, then?" said Sandy in her most pastoral tone. He gave her a few more details as she saw the lights of the other two ambulances. "Thank you for telling me that. They're going to do what we call a femoral stick to get some blood so we will know if you have enough oxygen in your system. You'll feel a little stick in your groin, but a tough *hombre* like you can handle it. I'll be back in a few minutes. I'm going to check on your homeys who just arrived. Anything you want me to tell them?"

He thought for a moment and then said, "Just tell them to hang tough."

131

"I can do that. You hang tough *tambien amigo*," she said as she headed for the door of Trauma Room 1, stripping off her gloves and other protective garb. She repeated the process of donning clean universal precaution gloves and plastic blouse in Trauma Room 2. Then she repeated the process and her *spiel* in the "curtain" area where the third patient was placed. He had a graze to his left shoulder and loose bowels, earning him the name "Poopy Pants" from the staff. *You gotta find the humor where you can in this business*, thought Chaplain (Resident) Sandra Womac, M. Div.

The second patient was much more problematic. He had lost consciousness on his way to the hospital, even though his injury was a "through and through" GSW to the left calf muscle. The medics were unable to ascertain the etiology of the LOC.

"Hurry and make sure the bleeding has stopped in his leg so we can get him to CT. I want his head scanned ASAP. I don't like not knowing what caused him to lose consciousness," directed Thaddeus T. Washington, MD. "Let's do it now, people. We aren't getting paid by the hour." The staff kicked into high gear and in a couple of minutes the patient was being moved to the CT scanner area. "Good work, people. Very good work," said Dr. Washington as he headed for the door to follow the gurney.

The next three hours were a blur for Sandy. Over thirty-five family members had arrived for the three patients. A few of the "bangers" also showed up, but security had kept them outside the building and frisked them for weapons. A small cache of pistols, knives, a pair of brass knuckles and a pair of numb-chucks were confiscated. Police arrived shortly after the ambulances and began to arrest those who were "carrying" illegally, i.e., all who previously had weapons. From a law enforcement perspective, it was a very good night.

By 0300 the patients were in the units to which they had been assigned and next of kin was with them. Sandy had learned from her first time as duty chaplain how *La Familia* manifests itself in the Hispanic culture. Frequently, she and her chaplain colleagues did as much crowd control as anything else because of the large number of family members who would come to the hospital to hold the vigil until some resolution of the case had occurred. They were now in the waiting areas. Most would leave later in the morning in time to get to work or school. The age span of these three families was eighty-seven years to six months.

"*Muy típico*," said Sandy, admiringly, to no one other than herself as she headed for the chaplain's duty room to log the most recent events of violence and mayhem. She made a half pot of coffee to get her caffeine level up before her adrenaline levels crashed. When she sat at the desk to record the cases, all she could think about was those few minutes in the treatment room with Dr. Sassmann. *Now what?* She thought. An hour later she had completed her entries and had even had a few minutes to reflect on what the breakfast might entail. The duty pager had been mercifully silent. She pushed herself away from the desk and willed herself to stand. *Guess I'd better make rounds through the ICUs and then the ED.*

The remainder of the early morning was uneventful. She had a couple of good conversations with staff members and even talked to a patient who couldn't sleep. A nurse had referred him to Sandy. He was a Vietnam Veteran and being in confined spaces, like hospital rooms, triggered his PTSD.

"Most of the time it doesn't bother me. But let me get somewhere I can't just get up and walk out of, and my anxiety starts to build. Once some wet behind the ears intern decided to take me off all my meds when he admitted me to rule out esophageal cancer. Twenty-four hours later, I was a total basket case. An Asian nurse walked into my room about 0500 in the morning. There were no lights on and before she knew what was happening, I was out of the bed and had her in a choke hold. I'm not proud of myself for that. It happened so fast I had no idea what I was doing. Not until the nurses' aid turned on the lights and yelled at me to stop. When I realized what was happening, I felt really ashamed. I must have apologized fifty times to that nurse over the next several days. Turns out she was Japanese, not Vietnamese. That intern's supervisor and I had a little pow wow the next day. I sure as hell hope that was the last time he ever pulled that lame brain stunt."

Sandy was too tired to practice active listening. She just let him talk

133

and said "Hmm" at appropriate times. When the first rays of sunrise began to streak the sky, the Vet thanked her for listening and told her to go see someone who needed her. The nurse thanked her for spending time with him.

"I know he's lonely. His wife left him a few years ago and he has been drinking pretty heavily, since." With these new staffing ratios, we just don't have time to sit and talk. If I'm not at the bedside giving meds, I'm at the computer logging everything I've just done. We never get caught up."

"Sounds like a vicious cycle, or at least a revolving door," reflected Sandy.

"Ain't it so, Chaplain. Ain't it so. I don't mean to be rude, but I have to get ready for report. Thanks again for seeing the Chief."

"Why do you call him, 'Chief'? Is he Native American?" asked Sandy.

"No," the nurse said with a chuckle. "He retired as a Chief Warrant Officer. Huey Dustoff pilot. He did two tours in Vietnam rescuing the wounded during fire fights. Guess he was pretty messed up when he got home from the last one. He's a frequent flier here in the MICU. He lives alone, has diabetes and that does not go well with the hooch, or vice versa." The nurse turned to go to the lounge for report with the shift coming on in a few minutes.

Maybe I should let Chaplain Anglemeyer or Chaplain Wilson know about 'The Chief.' They can give the secret handshake, as Ted says. Probably couldn't hurt. Sandy wrote notes for the two retired Army chaplains asking that one of them visit "The Chief." The duty pager went off as she was putting the identical notes in the appropriate "Pigeon holes" used to separate messages for the various chaplains. MEET ME IN THE ED IN 10 IF YOU STILL WANT BREAKFAST, KS. Her pulse quickened as she quickly erased the message. Just then, her relief walked through the door.

Jaime Martinez was a bit surprised when Sandy handed him the duty pager, said a quick "¡Hold!" picked up her purse and headed for the door. She didn't bother to tell him she was going to the Emergency Department. She stopped at a ladies' room to refresh her lipstick and shake a couple of tangles out of her hair.

14/0715 January 2006

"Hello," said Karl Sassmann, MD as Chaplain (Resident) Sandy Womac, M. Div. walked to the triage desk in the Emergency Department waiting room. His lips parted, just perceptibly, into a slight smile when he spoke. Sandy blushed as she glanced around to see if anyone was watching them.

"Let's get out of here, now!"

"I'll meet you at the Cracker Barrel on I-10 at Huebner," said Karl, now feeling a little self-conscious. "If that's okay with you. Do you like Cracker Barrel? If not, we could go somewhere else. Where would you like to go? I mean, well uh, I don't know too many other places around here. I just go there when I finish a shift. Is that okay? I...."

"I know this great place for breakfast about ten minutes from here," said Sandy, smiling at his discomfort and sudden lack of confidence.

"Oh, uh, okay. Where?"

"La Hacienda apartments on Babcock, number two forty-seven. I make a mean omelet. Regular or decaf coffee?"

"Regular." (Pause) "Are you sure?"

"Very. Here's my address," said Sandy as she scribbled something on a post-it note. "Hope you can read bad handwriting." With that she began walking toward the door, stopped, turned and said, "Count to a hundred by fives before you leave."

14/1840 January 2006

Chaplain (Resident) Jaime Martinez, M. Div. sat in the office of Clinical Chaplaincy Services on the tenth floor of Mercy Methodist Hospital in a near stupor. He was trying to write an entry into the duty log, with no success. Each time the pen touched the paper, he began to cry. At first it was just a few tears. About the fourth time he tried to write, he burst into sobs. *Chingada! Where the hell is all this coming from? He thought, when he had been able to stop crying. Am I losing it? What's wrong with me? It wasn't even that bad a shift.*

Jaime stood, stretched and began to walk around the room. As he did, he began to talk out loud. "What would Sister say right now? What would she tell me?" He continued to walk. When he sat down at the desk, he took a couple of deep breaths, exhaling slowly. "Ah, that's it. The old lady on the ortho unit." *Broken hip. She looked a little like Abuelita. That's how she died. Broken hip. Thought I had gotten over her death years ago. 'Obviously not,' as Sister would say. Damn. Didn't see that coming. That lady on Ortho looked so helpless and tired. Wouldn't surprise me if she's dead when I come back Monday. She's probably someone's grandmother, too. Wonder if they will miss her the way I miss Abuelita? Sometimes there's just too much death around here.*

He wiped his eyes, blew his nose and began to write about the referral he received from the nurse on 5-East (Ortho). The old woman had been a patient for several days and was not getting better, even though she should have been. *I think she has given up. She told me her husband died seven months ago. They had been married sixty-two years. Can't say as I blame her. I really don't think I did her any good. What's the point? Just what's the point of chaplaincy, anyway?*

"¡Hola, amigo!," a booming voice said. "How was your shift, *compadre*?" said Chaplain (Resident) John Wilson, D. Min.

"It was okay," lied Jaime. "Just finished writing it up. Glad to see you. I'm ready to get out of here." Pause. "Do you ever question whether or not we accomplish anything around here?"

"Not more than ten times a day. What's up? Have a case get to you?"

"No, just not feeling very efficient, or successful, or whatever the hell it is we're supposed to do around here."

"That's a big ten-four good buddy. I know just how you feel."

Jaime shot him a quick look.

136

"What I meant to say was, I hear the frustration you're feeling."

"Nice recovery. Sister Joyce would be proud of you for recognizing the error of your ways," said Jaime with a devilish grin.

"Never say you know just how someone else feels, because you don't," they said in unison, each mimicking the voice of their mentor, Sister Joyce. Then they laughed together.

"Hope you have a good shift, pilgrim!" said Jaime in his best (which was terrible) imitation of "The Duke." He left the office, thankful that he didn't have to be back for another thirty-eight hours. *But then, who's counting.*

14/1920 January 2006

"Who's a guy got to kiss to get an omelet around here?" asked Karl Sassmann, MD in mock sincerity.

"I don't think the word kiss is in that question, and we've already done the other, several times," replied Sandy. They had fallen into deep sleep after the first time they made the beast with two backs that morning. Each time they awoke, thereafter, they tried a varied form of copulation only to collapse into exhausted slumber.

"I'm starving," whined Karl. "If you want me to meet your wanton desires, I need to keep my strength up."

"It's not your strength I want you to keep up," Sandy said, giggling at her *double intender.*

"Nice talk for a CHAPLAIN," said Karl. "Aren't we breaking some kind of church rule? I mean, don't you have to wait until you're married to do what we've been doing? Don't you have to confess to that nun you report to? Oh crap. Do I go to hell for taking advantage of a 'baby chaplain?'"

"Screw you, Dr. Assmann!"

"Nice talk, Chaplain. And in case you have been asleep all day, you already did. 'Assmann?' Where did that come from? I've been nothing but nice to you ever since you showed up last June, all walking into walls and asking where the ladies room was. I have *always* been there to help you."

"Yeah, right," snorted Sandy. "And just for the record, we protestants don't take vows of chastity, or poverty for that matter, although you wouldn't notice based on our pay. Where does it say an humble servant of the Lord has to deprive herself of God's gift."

"You mean me?"

"Not even close. I mean our sexuality."

"I want to be a fly on the wall when you try to sell that to the good Sister. That dog won't hunt."

"Probably not," said Sandy with a slight sigh. She threw off the covers and walked into the bathroom, stark naked.

That is one fine looking derriere, thought the good Doctor Sassmann. He heard the toilet flush, then water running in the sink. Sandy appeared, put her hands on her hips and said, "I guess you still want me to fix you that breakfast I promised. Or would you rather have supper?" She was still totally naked.

I must have done something really wonderful in a former life to deserve this. Thank you, God. And I'm not being sacrilegious, thought Karl as Sandy slipped into an almost transparent robe and went into the kitchen. *Don't mess this up, Sassmann. This woman is very special. Very.*

15/0828 January 2006

"Good morning, Chief. I heard you were here and thought I'd drop by to say 'Howdy.'"

"Who's that?" said Chief Warrant Officer 4—Retired, USA Robert T. Slocum. He was apparently dazed by the intrusion.

Shit. He was asleep. Way to go, Chaplain Dumbass. "I apologize for waking you, Chief. The nurse said you were awake. How are you this morning?" said Chaplain (Resident) John Wilson, (LTC-RET, USA). "About time for 'stand to.'"

"You must be military, young man."

"Yes I am, Chief. U.S. Army Chaplain, Retired."

The grizzled Warrant tried to salute and that's when John noticed that he was in two point restraints. Assumedly, he had tried to pull out his IV tube during the night. A look of confusion and frustration was on his face.

"It's okay, Chief. Not necessary to salute, although I do appreciate your rendering of military courtesy. We can just keep it informal between a couple of old war horses. Heard you were a Huey driver in Vietnam. Dustoff."

"Yes sir. We lost a lot of good men over there. I just couldn't seem to save enough of them. The VC thought the red crosses on our birds were targets. We took a lot of rounds extracting our dead and wounded."

"Thank you for your service to our country and our comrades in arms, Chief. How many did you save?"

The old man had an expression of shock on his face. "I left Vietnam after my second tour in November '69. No one has ever asked me that question, until now."

"So how many did you save? I'll bet you it was a lot more than you lost. There are men walking the streets of our country, right now, who owe their lives to you and other Dustoff pilots."

Tears welled up in the Warrant Officer's eyes and ran down the sides of his face. "Thank you," he said when he had regained his composure and tried to come to a position of attention, in the bed. "I guess we did save some of them. I remember one young man…." His voice trailed off as he went back to Vietnam in his mind. His eyes grew wide and his face taut as he manually began to manipulate the cyclic and throttle of his Huey. "He was a black man from Georgia. Big as a house. Took two corpsmen and a great big white chaplain to carry him on a stretcher to the chopper. That Chaplain was something else. I remember he was saying that scripture about the shepherd and walking **through** the valley of

139

death. He always put special emphasis on that word, through."

"That was Chaplain Conrad N. "Connie" Walker. I worked for him in Germany, once. Recipient of the Silver Star and one hell of a good man. He was the chaplain I wanted to be when I grew up."

"I remember that name, now. Chaplain Connie. Anyway, this big black troop got thrown onto the bird just as I pulled pitch to get us the hell out of a hot LZ. We had AK-47 rounds pinging off the aircraft as we went light on the skids. This kid started to scream and it took my crew chief, no small guy himself, and a medic to hold him down while they got some morphine into him. He calmed down after a little and the rest of the flight was just balls to the wall to get back to the hospital as quickly as humanly possible."

"A few weeks later, the same guy walked into my hooch, stuck out his enormous paw and thanked me for saving his life. Called me a hero. Hell, I was just doing my job. I never had to back up to a pay table, but I sure never thought of myself as a hero, either. I got a Christmas card from him a couple of years later. Don't know how he got my address. He got out of the Army, married and they had a kid on the way. Pretty amazing, I guess."

"Tell me what's amazing?"

"That he would go to all that trouble to thank me for just earning my pay."

"Sounds like you made quite an impression on him, and vice versa. So how many did you save?"

"Hell Chappie, I got no idea. I did two tours."

"That's a lot of death and carnage you saw. That's also a lot of men you saved. You wouldn't be human if it hasn't affected you. How are the nightmares? Still having those?"

"Not more than once or twice a week. That seems to be one of the things my wife just couldn't handle. That and my drinking. I was up to a quart a day when she left me. I tried to quit several times. Even went to the VA for treatment, but nothing seemed to help. Now I've pickled my liver and the Docs say I'm dying. Hell of a mess, that war. Hell of a mess."

"Indeed it was, by all accounts. Again, thank you for your service." John paused, "I'd like you to do something while you're lying here in your bed, just thinking. I'd like you to remember as many of the guys you saved as you can."

"Hell, I can't do that. What difference would it make if I did?"

"Who's stopping you? I didn't say you have to remember all of them. I'll let you decide if it makes a difference. I need to go. My pager went off a couple of minutes, ago. I'll check in on you day after tomorrow. See you then, Chief. Anything I can do to be useful before I go?"

"No, but thanks for the visit, Chappie. Somehow, I feel a little better. More at peace, I guess."

"Good. See you Monday, Chief."

"When I have your wounded," the old man replied. It was a comment first made by Captain Charles Kelly, a Huey medevac pilot when ordered to evacuate a hot landing zone in Vietnam. It has since become the credo of that special breed of warriors, Dustoff.

As John turned to leave, he saw the old pilot's right arm pull against the restraint as he tried to salute. A tear ran down John's face as he walked out of the room, saying a prayer of thanksgiving for the warrior spirit and those willing to pay the high price of military service.

17/0725 January 2006

Chaplain (Resident) John Wilson (USA LTC-RET), D. Min., went to the sixth floor to check on "The Chief." He had been thinking about him during the quarterly, mandatory Day of Recollection, the day before. *Sure needed that. Can't believe the young bucks and buckettes get upset with Charles for requiring them to be there. Like they can just do this ministry day in and day out and never recharge their spiritual batteries. It was good to have the time to clear my head and focus on God and get out of the trenches for awhile. Makes me appreciate "El Jefe" even more.*

141

"How's 'The Chief' doing this morning?" asked John when the RN behind the nurses' station partition looked up from her computer.

She looked confused. "Robert Slocum, in thirty-six," added John.

"He died Sunday night. His nurse said it was a peaceful death, which shocked everyone. He was a real ring-tailed tooter of a patient. Couldn't please him if you hung him with a new rope," said the nurse. John stood in stunned silence.

When he collected himself, he said, somewhat lamely, "Thanks. I didn't think he would go so quickly."

"Chaplain, he had been self-medicating for years." She mimed taking a long swig from a bottle. "He's been in and out of here for several years. Apparently, he had a pretty good job at one time and still has good insurance. That's why he was here. Most of the vets like him are at Audie Murphy VA Hospital."

"Yeah, the government pretty much screwed the pooch on the way they didn't take care of the Vietnam vets. Damned shame, if you ask me, and damned unfair," said John. His thoughts were a long way from his body. He was in a Bagdad battalion aid station looking at the mangled bodies of America's youth. He felt his body begin to tremble. "See you around the campus," he said to the nurse as he turned quickly and headed for the day room. He could feel the tears welling up in him and he needed some privacy to process this most recent grief and some of the old ones.

CHAPTER 10

18/1530 January 2006

"Chaplain, the wife is here," said Chaplain (Resident) Jaime Martinez, M. Div. to Charles McRae who had just walked out of the restricted area of the operating suites. He was wearing black hospital scrubs with his name and a cross embroidered in gold on the left chest pocket. He also wore booties, cap and surgical mask. He had pulled the mask down so that it hung around his neck, rather than cover his nose and mouth. He had selected the main OR for his clinical site "Just to remind himself of why he was REALLY in the hospital business," as he liked to explain to his boss, Bill Groene, FACHE, CEO of MMHS when questioned. He used the medical model of physicians continuing to function as physicians, even when they were in administrative roles as employees of the hospital. It also helped him model for the Residents what clinical chaplaincy is about or at least his idea of it.

The first time he shared an event that took place in the OR with Beth, she asked why he was there. "The patients are all asleep."

"I'm not there for the patients. I'm there for the staff. That's our first responsibility. Patients come second—in the normal course of things. Families come third. Of course, that changes, based on who is in crisis at the moment."

"I guess that follows some form of logic," said Beth, slowly. "Still, it seems the most important group of people is the patients."

"Patients come and go. And we are there for them, but it's the staff that requires our ongoing attention. When we help them through a crisis or a problem, we are helping to reduce turnover. When we use our wonderful listening and communication skills, not to mention conflict resolution strategies, we can significantly reduce the stress level on a unit. That translates to a positive impact on the bottom line. The bean counters love us, or are at least they are less intolerant, when that happens."

"You think in strange ways Dr. McRae," Beth said with a smile.

"Why, thank you, Dr. McRae. You have no idea just how warm and fuzzy that makes me feel."

"Jaime, I think we have a problem."

"Sir?" said Jaime with a confused look on his face.

"I came on as duty chaplain at 1300 and we had a GSW in the ED. I met his "wife" a few minutes after they moved him to the OR. She's in the family room. I was just checking on how his procedure was going so I could give her a report, when I bumped into you. You're through with your IPR (Interpersonal Relationship) session?"

"Yes, sir. What would you like for me to do?" asked Jaime.

"Well since Chaplain Allison is off this p.m., hence my carrying the duty pager, you are the stuckee. I'll give you report on the patient and you can start taking care of 'Wife number two' until we can sort this out. Okay?"

"Yes, sir. Where do you want me to put her?"

"Let's check with Brenda. She can probably give us one of the consultation rooms. Just remember, young Chaplain, that competent unit secretaries, like Brenda, have **all** the power as well as the most accurate information. You heard it here first." Jaime smiled only slightly as he began trudging toward the unit secretary's desk with the enthusiasm of a man going to the gallows. *What a great learning experience for an enterprising young chaplain resident*, thought Charles. *He'll laugh about this next week.*

"What I have determined, young Chaplain," said Charles McRae, D. Min., BCC, LPC to Chaplain (Resident) Jaime Martinez, M. Div., "Is that wife number one is the common law wife and wife number two is the estranged legal wife. The latter has not talked to her husband or three adult children for over eight years. That was shortly after said husband began having an affair with wife number one. Obviously, wife number two couldn't take a joke when her husband became unfaithful. Some women just have no sense of humor," said McRae with a straight face.

Jaime tried, unsuccessfully, to not laugh. "So what do we do now?" asked Jaime. "She, wife number two, is really angry about the other woman being here and is demanding that the mistress leave. She even threatened to call security."

"Interestingly enough, that's not going to happen. The children are on the side of the common law 'wife.' They've been living together for the last eight years which in Texas qualifies her as the spouse. Sounds like wife number two is SOL. That means 'Sure Out of Luck,' young chaplain," said Dr. McRae solemnly. Again, Jaime tried to stifle a laugh. "Please go tell wife number two that you will take her in to see her 'husband' when he gets to his bed in SICU. Of course, that will be after I take wife number one and the adult children in to see him. Does that sound like a plan to you?"

"Yes sir."

"How are you going to handle the situation, Jaime?" asked Charles.

"Sir?"

"What's your plan of ministry with the lady you are caring for?" asked Charles, quietly.

Jaime paused for the better part of thirty seconds. "I plan to give her the information you suggested and then stay with her until her sister gets here. She's on the way. I was in the room when Mrs. Gomez called her. There was a lot of discussion about how she is the one who is entitled to receive the life insurance if he dies and then a lot more about his lack

145

of character and, as you would say, Sir, his ancestry. She was not kind."

"What's your take on all that?" asked Charles.

"Frankly, Sir, I think she's just in it for the money. Clearly, she has no concern for the man and would prefer that he die so she can get the insurance money. She's really not a very nice woman, Sir."

"And how does that inform your ministry?"

"As I said, I plan to stay with her until the sister arrives. Then I'll excuse myself to make rounds until you page me that it's okay to take her into the Unit. After that, I'll just play it by ear," said Jaime.

"Is that like being led by the Spirit, Chaplain?" Charles said with a slight smile.

"Yes Sir, that's what I meant to say," Jaime replied quickly. He was also grinning.

"We wouldn't want to disappoint Sister, now would we, young Chaplain?"

"Oh, no sir. Far from it. I'm just here to follow the Spirit wherever 'She' leads me," said Jaime, now chuckling.

"Good plan. By the way, sounds like this will make a great verbatim. This kind of thing doesn't happen often." Charles paused and then added, "I'm glad you're on the team, Jaime. You do a good job. Drop by the office when you finish with wife number two and I'll buy you a cup of coffee. I'd like to hear how it turns out. I'll page you when I've taken wife number one in to see Mr. Gomez."

"Yes Sir," Jaime said as he turned to walk away. Charles thought Jaime had a grown a couple of inches since their conversation. *Guess I should offer compliments more often. Seems to have a positive effect on the troops*, thought Charles as he turned to go to the Family Room.

18/1720 January 2006

Jaime stood in the office door as he waited patiently for Dr. Charles McRae to look up from his computer screen and acknowledge his presence. The office was quite small by corporate standards. The furniture was hand-me-down and the carpet was a bit worn. The entire suite was modest, especially the conference room. In order to get the entire PCS team in it, the chairs had to be removed and everyone had to stand.

Several years before the partnership which formed the System, the Senior Leadership Team of Mercy Methodist Hospital had moved into temporary office trailers during a renovation of the first floor, which housed the executive suite. Midway into the renovation, the CEO, CFO, COO and CNE consensed that it was more pragmatic to use the renovated space for other agencies and departments while they remained in the trailers. In time, it became a badge of honor, or at least humility, to not use funds on a well-appointed executive suite. It also led to not a few quietly spoken comments about who of the hospital personnel were the trailer trash.

This also became a minor contention in the blending of cultures as the senior leadership teams of the other, and smaller, four hospitals owned by the for profit company slowly lost their cherry wood furniture and large offices through an ongoing process of renovations and relocations.

"Jaime, come in, come in. Just made a fresh pot of coffee. Would you like a cup?"

"Yes sir, that would be good. It's been a long day and my caffeine level is a bit low. Would you like a warm-up on yours, sir?" asked Jaime.

Charles slid his cup toward the Resident as he said, "Just give me a second to finish this email to Bill Groene." Jaime returned with the two mugs of coffee, just as Charles was closing his laptop. "So, how did it go with the bereaved wife number two?" The young chaplain sat in one of the two waiting room chairs which were against the same wall Charles' desk was facing. Much of the remainder of the office walls were covered with shelves, laden with too many books per shelf and a few photos and other knick knacks. A large painting of a pastoral scene and a print of a Texas country side by Slaughter, a famous local artist decorated the walls. Charles swung his office chair, and therefore himself, to face Jaime.

147

"Actually it wasn't nearly as bad as I feared it would be. But then, according to Sister, it rarely is. As soon as the doctor told her that her husband did well in surgery and his injuries were not life threatening, she and her sister left the hospital—in a huff. The latter arrived just a few minutes after I had moved the estranged wife to an empty patient room. By the way, Brenda was very helpful and very kind to me. She seemed to pick up on my elevated stress level. I appreciated that."

"Did I mention that good unit secretaries are psychic?" asked Charles.

"No, sir, but I believe you. I thought I was being very professional and was modeling 'calm, cool and collected'. Guess I wasn't."

"Perhaps," responded Charles with a wry smile on his face. *You looked like you were going to your own execution, Chaplain*, thought Charles. "So she didn't wait around to see her beloved husband? I would be led to believe that your initial assessment reference the insurance money was accurate. As my friend, the good Rabbi Leinwand says, 'Where there's a will, there's usually a family'."

"Yes sir, that pretty well sums it up. How did it go with the other wife?" asked Jaime in a casual way.

Is this kid trying to do pastoral care on me? Pause. *Good for him. ¡El tiene juevos grandes!* "She was within-normal-limits the entire time. Very relieved when the doctor told her he would probably survive, as were the adult children. She also shared more history about the 'arrangement' of their relationship and events leading up to it. Not a pretty picture. I got the distinct impression that today was not the first time wife number two was not a pleasant person. But then, perhaps wife number one failed to mention some of her less sterling attributes as well as the husband in question." He was smiling as he said it and Jaime smiled, also. "If it weren't for people, our job would be quite easy and boring."

"Yes sir. So how was it to be back in the clinical saddle, so to speak?"

"I enjoy clinical work, Jaime." *Is he doing his pastoral care thing again?* "It keeps me grounded and feels a whole lot more like ministry than going

148

to meetings and moving paper from one side of my desk to the other."

"That can get boring pretty quickly, can't it, sir? I don't envy you your job."

"Yes it can, until I remember that if I don't do what I do, you and the other clinicians can't do what you do. I guess that is in some convoluted way; ministry too. On the other hand, clinical chaplaincy is a young person's game. I'm getting too old to be on the floors all the time. I also enjoy helping to educate the corporate types on what this is all about and why PCS is a value added department. There's just nothing like watching the light bulb come on when I'm explaining what we really do and how different that is from Pastor I'm-so-heavenly-minded-I'm-no-earthly-good dumbing around the halls in search of one of his parishioners."

"Sounds like you get a lot of energy from that, sir."

Good active listening, Chaplain. "Yes I do. Helps make the Mickey Mouse stuff and the politics more tolerable. Plus, it gives me a chance to get to know young Chaplains such as yourself, Jaime. I don't care what Sister says about you, I think you do a good job and I'm glad to have you on the team." The young man smiled and blushed at the same time.

"I guess I'd better be going, sir, unless you have something else for me," Jaime said as he stood.

"No, that's about it. Just wanted to check your pulse and see how things turned out for you. Enjoy your evening, Jaime. Please give my regards to Maria and tell her it's my fault you're late getting home. See you tomorrow."

"Yes sir. Thank you, sir," said Jaime as he grabbed his cup and, nodding toward Dr. McRae's and seeing his nod, took them both to the kitchenette. His feet didn't touch the ground until he got to the parking garage. *To be affirmed by Dr. McRae like that is great. Wow, I had no idea he even knew who I was, much less what my wife's name is. Can't wait to tell her.*

That's one fine young Chaplain. I'd take a dozen of him, thought Charles as he began to pack his soft leather brief case.

Karl Sassmann, MD took a long pull on his beer, sat it down on the coffee table, tried to disguise a belch and asked, "So what did Sister Jean say when you told her?"

"It's Sister Joyce, and she didn't say much of anything. She just listened. I don't think she was surprised. Maybe she saw it coming." Pause. "I sure didn't," said Sandy, reflectively. "I was convinced you hated me." Pause. "She did ask if we practiced safe sex. I wasn't ready for that. I thought she would pull out her ruler and wrap me across my knuckles, or whatever the equivalent of that is in CPE Speak."

"What's to be critical of? We're both consenting adults. This is 2006 for Christ's sake," said Karl with some disgust in his voice. "She didn't try to guilt you, even just a little?"

"No. Before the session ended she suggested we offer a short prayer of thanksgiving for your coming into my life."

"Really? Now I'm shocked. Although, I have usually thought of myself as God's gift to women," Karl said with a twinkle in his eye.

"Not what she was talking about, Dr. Assman, although I do agree with her theology. All kidding aside, my love, you are an answer to my prayers. I've been so lonely for so long. Being the solo pastor in a small South Texas town puts a serious crimp in one's love life. So where do we go from here?"

Karl looked around Sandy's apartment. It was a study in elegant simplicity. She was careful not to flaunt her family's wealth, especially among her chaplain colleagues, but she had used some of it, at least her trust fund payments to purchase quality furniture and accent pieces. Most of the paintings were originals by local artists. Her palatte was royal blue, cream and gold. Each room had an accent wall of royal blue with the other walls painted cream. The trim was also cream. The gold was a highlight in the upholstery of the couch, love seat and window treatments. The art work brought out those colors. The last few days he had found the apartment relaxing and Sandy's company very stimulating on several levels. They acted like two adolescents in heat. And yet, he recognized a depth in their relationship unlike any he had experienced.

"Dinner is served," announced Sandy as she carried a plate of homemade fried chicken to the table. Mashed potatoes, "little green peas," (Green Giant Le Sueur very young small sweet peas), homemade rolls and cream gravy sat steaming on the table. Large glasses filled with sweetened iced tea were next to her "everyday" china, *Petite Fleur* by Villaroy & Boch. Slices of lemon and lime along with sprigs of fresh sweet mint completed the setting.

"All this and great sex, too?" he asked as he walked to the table, taking the last swig of his long neck Lone Star. "I just may have to start hanging out with you on a more regular basis."

"Don't get your hopes up, our schedules for the next six months are not going to be that compatible. Although, I'm not opposed to seeing you when I can work you into my busy schedule. I have souls to save and the afflicted to comfort, you know," quipped Sandy as a broad smile spread across her face. After they were both seated, she took his hand and said, "Bless O Lord these gifts which we are about to receive from thy bounty, through Christ our Lord, Amen."

"Pass the potatoes please," Karl said as he used his fork to spear the largest piece of chicken on the platter. "Smells great. Thank you, my love. I appreciate the lengths to which you go to keep up my strength. Frankly, your appetites in the bedroom, or wherever, can be quite exhausting."

"Are you complaining or bragging, Dr. Assman?" asked Sandy, sweetly.

"Actually, I'm a breast man, as you can see," he said while holding up the piece of chicken he had speared. Sandy rolled her eyes at him. "You're sassing me, right? You sass the very man, a Medical Doctor no less, who has liberated you from your lonely nights and extreme wantonness? Your problem, young Chaplain Resident is you have no appreciation, much less, thankfulness for the gift the Almighty has provided you. Namely, *'moi,'*" said Karl in a most sonorous tone as he stuffed a large bite

151

of chicken dipped in mashed potatoes and gravy into his mouth.

"So where to from here?" asked Sandy.

Karl became serious and looked deeply into her eyes. "I think I am falling in love with you, Sandy. I have never felt this away about anyone, before." Pause. "Let's see how we do with the craziness of our schedules and work the next six months and plan from there. I want to be with you as much as I possibly can, but I fear that's not going to be nearly enough. Let's plan a trip for when you graduate and I start my next rotation. I have two weeks off beginning June fifth."

A tear ran down Sandy's cheek as she caressed his hand. "I love you so much, Karl. You are everything I have ever wanted. Thank you for caring about me and wanting to be with me. You will never know how much that means." Pause. "I accept your offer. Maybe we can go to Midland for Easter so my parents can meet you."

20/2300 January 2006

Chaplain (Resident) Jaime Martinez, M. Div. felt his pager vibrate as he was about to enter the SICU. He stopped in the middle of the hallway and read the script on the small electronic box. "PLEASE RETURN TO 5W." He felt a slight "bump" of adrenalin as he turned on his heel and began walking briskly to the stairs. He dropped two floors and walked to the nurses' station. An attractive young charge nurse looked at him with relief in her eyes as she said, "She's just about gone, Chaplain."

"Thank you for paging me. I really appreciate it," he said as he turned to walk to the room of the patient he had been asked by the nurse to visit earlier in the evening. Jaime had found that staff frequently forgot to page him as he requested when he was needed. It was quite frustrating after expending time and energy with a family or patient and then not be called when something critical was occurring.

Jaime wrapped softly on the door to the patient room as he walked in to 523. The lights were low and the husband, two adult daughters, their husbands and adult son were standing around the bed of their wife/mother/mother-in-law. She was an eighty-four year old Caucasian woman who had been actively dying of colorectal cancer, the last three days. Jaime recognized the "Q sign" she was making with her open mouth and tongue to the lower left side of it. He felt guilty for doing so, because it was an inside joke among hospital personnel. Patients frequently presented that way shortly before expiration.

The old farmer looked completely lost. He had seen death in various forms in his eighty-eight years of living on his family's homestead. He told Jaime he had never done anything but "Be a sod buster," when the young chaplain had visited earlier in the day. "Me and Martha was married sixty-seven years ago, last June. We waited to get married until she graduated High School. We'd been dating for over a year. Well, writing each other. I knew I was going to marry her the first time I saw her. I was home on leave from the Army and went to the High School football game there in town and she was a cheerleader. She was just a kid in Junior High when I left for the Army. Now, she was all grown up. That was 1938. I'll never forget what an angel she was jumping up and down on the side of the field," he said with watery eyes. Jaime had become a bit misty-eyed himself as the old timer told his story.

Jaime quickly shook hands with the old man and walked to the patient's side. He bent over, close to her ear and said, "Martha, this is Chaplain Martinez. I'm here with your family and I'm going to look after them when you're gone. I'm going to take good care of them." Pause. "Martha, I want to say one of the psalms with you and I want you to listen to the promises that are in it." Jaime began to recite the twenty-third psalm. "The Lord is my shepherd, I shall not want. He maketh me to lie down in green pastures...." When he finished, he gently placed his hand on her head and stroked it a couple of times. "Those promises are for you and for your family. You can trust them now and always." He discreetly wiped a tear from his eye as he stood. He stepped next to the farmer and gently put his hand on his shoulder. He began to remember the stories the old man had told him earlier. He felt he should be doing something, but he didn't know what it was. So, he just stood there with the family in silence.

Jaime was pulled from his thoughts as he realized Martha had not recently taken a breath. He counted to twenty and she had still not breathed. As he looked more closely, he saw that her complexion was beginning to change. He stepped a little closer and touched her hand. She was dead. He reached for the nurse call button and engaged it. A moment later, the young RN walked in, listened with her stethoscope and shook her head. She confirmed what Jaime already knew, expressed her condolences and said, "I'll call the doctor. I'm very sorry." Pause. "Can I get you anything?"

Each of the family members silently shook their heads as they dabbed at their eyes with readily supplied tissues. The old man just stood like a statue, looking at his wife's body. One by one the children quietly said their good-byes and left the room to give their father some alone time with his wife. When they were all gone, and the old man continued to just stare, Jaime asked, "Is there anything you would like to say to Martha? It's okay to talk to her, or touch her." Silence. After a moment, when Jaime couldn't tolerate his own anxiety and helplessness, he said, "Would you like for me to say a prayer before we leave?"

The old man turned on his heel and left the room without saying a word. *Oh crap, I've done it now. McRae and Sister both have told us, several times, that prayer isn't what you do when you don't know what else to do. Did I piss him off? Was I too abrupt?*

Just then, Jaime heard the farmer say in what for him was an uncommonly loud voice, "Children, children come here. The preacher's going to say grace over Momma!" Jaime didn't know whether to laugh or cry. The family filed in and Jaime offered a prayer of thanksgiving for Martha's life and the love she had given her family through the years. After the "Amen," the children began to gather up their belongings and a couple of the pots of flowers. Jaime led the old man out into the hallway and walked them to the elevator. He rode down with them to the ground floor and walked them to the front door of the hospital.

He felt the usual emptiness and helplessness as they left and he turned to go back to 5W. *Need to check the staff's pulse so they can do it all again.* As he trudged to the elevators, he began to think about what the old man had said in his total lack of religious sophistication. "The preacher's going to say grace over Momma." And then it hit him: He was here to say Grace over the tragedies and crises of life.

GLOSSARY

02-Oxygen

AADC-Adjusted Average Daily Census, daily patient census plus prorated number of outpatients per day

ABICU-Adult Burn Intensive Care Unit

ACPE-Association of Clinical Pastoral Education

ADC-Average Daily Census, the number of patients in the hospital in a twenty-four hour period

Anterior-the front of a body or its parts

APC-Association of Professional Chaplains

BAMC-Brooke Army Medical Center

BCC-Board Certified Chaplain

CCS-Clinical Chaplaincy Services

CCU-Cardiac Care Unit

CEO-Chief Executive Officer

CEU-Continuing Education Units

CFO-Chief Financial Officer

CNA-Certified Nurses' Aid

CNE-Chief Nursing Executive

Code Blue-Procedural alert for cardiac and/or respiratory arrest

COO-Chief Operating Officer

CPA-Certified Public Accountant

CPE-Clinical Pastoral Education

CPR-Cardio Pulmonary Resuscitation

CT scan-Computerized Tomography

D. Min.-Doctor of Ministry

Diverticulitis-Inflammation of one or more diverticula

DNA-Deoxyribonucleic acid

DOD-Department of Defense

EAP-Employee Assistance Program

ED-Emergency Department

EMT-Emergency Medical Technician

ER-Emergency Room

FMLA-Family Medical Leave Act

FTE-Full Time Equivalency

FTO-Flexible Time Off

FY-Fiscal Year

GSW-Gunshot wound

HIPAA-Health Insurance Portability and Accountability Act

HR-Human Resources

HSI-Health Source, Inc.

IPR-Interpersonal relationship group

ISR-Institute of Surgical Research

IV-Intravenous catheter

JCAHO-Joint Commission on Accreditation of Hospital Organizations

JD-Doctor of Jurisprudence

LMFT-Licensed Marriage and Family Therapist

LOC-Loss of consciousness

LPC-Licensed Professional Counselor

LVN-Licensed Vocational Nurse

LZ-Landing Zone

MD-Medical Doctor

MICU-Medical Intensive Care Unit

MMHS-Mercy Methodist Healthcare System

MRI-Magnetic Resonance Imaging

MS-Master of Science

MVA-Motor vehicle accident

NACC-National Association of Catholic Chaplains

OR-Operating room

PA-Professional Association

PA-Public address system

PCC-Pastoral Counseling Center

PCS-Pastoral Care Services

Pedi-Relating to children or pediatrics

PE-Pulmonary embolism

PET scan-Position Emission Tomography

PhD-Doctor of Philosophy

Posterior-the back of a body or its parts

PRN-Latin phrase meaning as the circumstances arise or as needed

Ps. D.-Doctor of Psychology

PT-Physical Therapist/therapy

PTSD-Post Traumatic Stress Disorder

PTS-Post Traumatic Stress

RCSC-Rape Crisis Services Center

RN-Registered Nurse

RT-Respiratory Therapist/therapy

S.I.T.-Supervisor In Training

SAFE-Sexual Assault Forensic Evidence

SAPD-San Antonio Police Department

SICU-Surgical Intensive Care Unit

SOB-Shortness of breath

STAT-Latin word *statim*, meaning immediately

SWTC-Southwest Texas Conference (of the United Methodist Church)

USA -United States Army

UTSA-University of Texas, San Antonio

VC-Vietcong

Vital Signs-Pulse, blood pressure, temperature

VP-Vice President